The DRAGON TREE

THE HALL FAMILY CHRONICLES

THE DRAGON TREE

JANE LANGTON

The Hall Family Chronicles

■ HarperCollins*Publishers*

Library of Congress Cataloging-in-Publication Data is available.
ISBN 978-0-06-082341-2 (trade bdg.)—ISBN 978-0-06-082342-9 (lib. bdg.)

Typography by Larissa Lawrynenko
1 2 3 4 5 6 7 8 9 10

First Edition

For Nathan, James and Paul

Mythology is . . . the great dragon-tree of the Western Isles, as old as mankind.

—HENRY DAVID THOREAU

Contents

The Dragon Tree

NO PRINCE EITHER

"CONGRATULATIONS, DEAR Mortimer and Margery!"

Annabelle Broom, the real estate lady, had come to welcome Mr. and Mrs. Mortimer Moon to their new Concord home. As the moving van drove away from No. 38 Walden Street, the proud owners stood smiling on their very own front porch.

"Why, thank you, Annabelle!" said Mrs. Moon, beaming at her over an armful of teddy bears.

"Oh, don't thank me," said Annabelle, shaking her head. "I've also come to warn you about the neighbors."

"The neighbors?" Mrs. Moon glanced nervously at the house next door, where a lanky redheaded boy was loping up the walk.

Her husband frowned. "What's the matter with the neighbors?"

"Oh, they're all right, really," said Annabelle. "In fact Mr. Hall is supposed to be this big important professor." She rolled her eyes comically. "But as for the children!" She moved closer and lowered her voice to a whisper. "Dear people, I must warn you, because I see you have a teenage daughter."

"You don't mean Emerald?" Margery Moon laughed merrily. "She's not our daughter. She's my husband's second cousin, three times removed."

"The poor child was an orphan, you see," explained Mortimer Moon. "So we took her in."

"How generous of you!" said Annabelle.

"And not only that." Margery cuddled her teddy bears. "We gave her a job as our maid-of-all-work."

"How kind of you!" said Annabelle as the screen door opened and a pale girl stepped out on the porch.

"Oh, Emerald," said Mrs. Moon, "I want you to be extremely careful unloading the car. My crystal goblets are extremely fragile."

The girl said, "Okay, Mrs. Moon," and hurried down the steps.

Annabelle watched with narrowed eyes, noting the way the girl's yellow hair floated out behind her. "Well, just the same, a word of warning. You see, there are three children in the house next door."

Mortimer Moon raised his eyebrows. "Juvenile delinquents, you mean?"

"Well, no, I wouldn't say that. The girls are fairly harmless, I suppose, and anyway the older girl's away in Paris, France. Georgie, the little one, is fairly harmless. But there is also a son named Edward." Annabelle corrected herself. "Or perhaps he's a nephew. Whatever."

"He's the delinquent?" Margery Moon turned her head and stared fearfully at the neighboring house, where the redheaded boy was lingering on the porch with his hands in his pockets.

"Not delinquent exactly," said Annabelle. "But

he's part of a gang, a whole crowd of kids. The rabble, I call them. As far as I know, Edward has never actually been in trouble with the police, but . . ."

"But what?" said Margery and Mortimer together.

"Just take care, that's all. I urge you to keep an eye on your maid, Ruby."

"Emerald," corrected Margery.

"Of course. I knew it was some precious stone." Then Annabelle spoke firmly. "If I were you, I'd forbid her to have anything to do with those people. Anything *what-so-ever*."

"Goodness me!" Margery stared keenly at her husband's second cousin, three times removed, as she heaved a large box out of the trunk of the car.

"And there's something else about Number Forty Walden Street," said Annabelle. "I suppose I should have warned you about it before."

"Warned us about what?" said Mortimer Moon, frowning.

But then his wife screeched at the maid-of-all-work as she staggered up the walk with the box. "Be careful, Emerald!"

just happened to be feeding Aunt Alex's chickens.

Normally it was Georgie's job, but today he had offered to help. "Well, okay," said Georgie, handing him the pail.

But Eddy wasn't paying attention to the chickens. After tossing a handful of cracked corn over the fence, he turned to wave at the girl with yellow hair and shout, "Hi there!"

But she only gave him a frightened glance, then turned her back and threw herself at the lawnmower, shoving it rapidly away and vanishing behind the far side of the house.

"She's stuck-up, I guess," murmured Eddy, crestfallen.

"She has green eyes," whispered Georgie.

Emerald nodded and struggled up the steps. But as she tottered across the porch, Mrs. Moon shook a warning finger and said, "Those goblets must be washed at once, do you hear me, Emerald?"

Clutching the heavy box, Emerald turned the handle of the screen door with two fingers, bumped the door open with her knee, and kept it open by leaning against it. "Okay, Mrs. Moon," she said, edging sideways into the house.

"And don't forget, Emerald," exclaimed Mrs. Moon, raising her voice, "the shelves must be scrubbed first."

"Right." Emerald gasped, feeling the box begin to slip and taking a firmer hold.

Then Mr. Moon shouted through the screen door, "Oh, and Emerald, when you're finished in the kitchen, please mow the backyard."

Emerald leaned against the kitchen counter, set down the box, and took a deep breath, remembering an old story about a ragged girl, a stepmother, a couple of stepsisters, a fairy godmother, and a prince.

In her own case the stepsisters were missing

and there was certainly no fairy godmother. And no prince either.

Back on the front porch, Annabelle Broom said crisply, "Mr. and Mrs. Moon, do I have your full attention?"

"Certainly," said Mortimer Moon.

"Because there's something else you should know about the house next door."

"What?" said Margery and Mortimer together.

"It's jam-packed with something truly horrible." Annabelle looked at her watch, squealed, "Sorry, gotta go," and scuttled down the porch steps.

"Wait a minute!" shrieked Margery Moon.

"Jam-packed with what?" bellowed Mortimer Moon.

Annabelle called something over her shoulder as she galloped to her car, but they didn't hear. "What did you say?" screamed Margery.

Leaping in behind the wheel, Annabelle slammed the car door, leaned out the car window, and shouted her warning again as she zoomed away. This time they heard it clearly: "*Watch out for weirdness buildup*."

THE STUCK-UP GIRL

AS SHE LUGGED the box of glassware into the house, Emerald heard the news about the scary boy, and then the warning about his dangerous house. Therefore, as she trundled the lawnmower out of the garage, she was careful not to glance at the alarming porches and threatening gables and bulging tower of the house next door.

But the scary boy who lived in the house was not afraid to look at his new neighbor. While Emerald leaned forward to push the lawnmower through the thick grass, then heaved it backwards and swerved it around bushes and trees, Eddy Hall

3

THE RABBLE

ANNABELLE BROOM HAD CALLED them a
rabble. But the family at No. 40 Walden
Street was really just an ordinary mixture of
human beings, chickens, and a cross-eyed cat—
unless you also counted the statuary.

1. Professor Frederick Hall was the head of
   the household. Part of the time Uncle
   Fred was a Concord selectman, but most
   of the time he sat at his desk writing a
   book about that great genius Henry
   Thoreau, who had lived down the road at
   Walden Pond a long time ago and written

a masterpiece called *Walden*. Everybody expected Uncle Fred's book to be another masterpiece—that is, if he could ever calm down enough to finish it.

2. Professor Alexandra Hall. Aunt Alex was another fan of Henry Thoreau, but instead of springing joyfully out of her chair to quote magnificent passages, she kept them in her heart.

3. Eleanor Hall was their niece. At the moment, Eleanor was studying abroad, but she wrote excited letters home: *"Paris is just so incredibly awesome!"* or *"Paris really sucks!"*

4. Her brother, Edward Hall, wore a gold stud in one ear and his baggy pants hung from his hip bones, but, delinquent or not (probably not), he was a big man at high school. Eddy was cool, really cool, a noisy comedian who liked to talk about himself in the third person:

"Gallantly our hero took out the garbage."

"With saintly benevolence our hero

assisted his aged aunt."

"*Modestly our hero bowed to the cheering crowd.*"

5. Georgie Hall was a sixth grader in the Alcott School. Georgie was a quiet and obedient little girl, but when she made up her mind about something important, there was no stopping her. Once she had walked all the way to Washington to talk to the President. She had begun her march all by herself, but by the time her great Children's Crusade reached the White House, it was sixteen thousand strong. To Uncle Fred, Georgie was like a force of nature.

6. Henry Thoreau had been dead for years, but in a way he too was a resident of No. 40 Walden Street. Uncle Freddy's hero was only a bust on a tall stand in the front hall, but the gaze of his plaster eyes seemed to pierce the wall as though he could see all the way to Walden Pond, where long ago the real Henry had written his famous book.

7. The other piece of statuary was a tall bronze woman on the newel post of the staircase, a majestic sort of light fixture. The word TRUTH was inscribed across her metal dress like a motto, as though she were saying, "Now hear this!"

8. The rest of the rabble didn't live at No. 40 Walden Street. They were a flock of noisy kids in the neighborhood: Eddy's friends Oliver Winslow and Hugo Von Bismarck and Georgie's classmates Frieda Caldwell, Cissie Updike, Otis Fisher, Sidney Bloom, and Rachel Adzarian. After school they milled around in each other's houses and messed up their mothers' kitchens and watched TV in each other's living rooms and drove their parents crazy.

9. And then there was the Oversoul. Well, it's probably silly to call the Oversoul a member of the household, but Uncle Fred could feel it looming over the roof in a kindly cloud. No wonder he was so often carried away by fits of excitement. Not

only did the Oversoul shower him with lofty thoughts from above, but the statuary in the front hall did the same thing, only sideways, as though reaching out to pluck his sleeve whenever he walked by.

10. Last of all, there was the house itself. Was No. 40 Walden Street really infected with "weirdness buildup"? Or was it filled to overflowing with something else entirely?

4

LEFTOVER MAGIC

Yes, THERE WAS something else. It was leftover magic.

Uncle Fred was too busy writing his great book to think about it much, but Aunt Alex was aware of it all the time.

In the kitchen, for instance, she sometimes had to clap a lid over her pot of soup to keep sparkles from falling into it from the enchanted air. In the front hall the radiator sometimes rattled as if it were trying to tell her something, and Henry's plaster lips often seemed to whisper, *Listen, listen,* and the lamp in the metal hand of the lady on the newel post glittered like a star. Even the laundry on the back porch—Eddy's pants and Uncle Freddy's shirts—sometimes danced as if they were alive.

And as for the attic! Once in a while Aunt Alex climbed the attic stairs just to look around and remember, because so many wonders were packed away up there, such as Eddy's mysterious bicycle and Georgie's American flag and the snowflake wedding dress and the glowing rubber ball and the windows that once upon a time had flashed and twinkled like a diamond.

All these marvels were out-of-date, stored away and forgotten. But the house itself did not forget, because it was still bewitched—not with a weird decay like mildew, but with something like a healthy flow of blood in the wiring or a rush of water singing in the pipes.

The leftover magic was now so thick that it drenched the walls, made its way through the clapboards, and dripped down on Aunt Alex's flower bed. Soon her trumpet lilies were hooting softly and

17

her marigolds glimmered in the dark.

Farther and farther spread the spell of the enchanted house, moving underground through dirt and rock, heading northward in the direction of the house next door.

5

THE SWELLING IN THE GROUND

"E DDY, DEAR," SAID Aunt Alex, "you mustn't stare."

"Oh, right." Eddy turned away from the window, but every now and then he couldn't help taking another look at the neighboring house.

The stuck-up green-eyed girl did not appear again, but Mr. Moon was everywhere at once.

He was a hard worker, you could see that. Every time Eddy twitched a curtain aside he saw Mr. Moon hurrying briskly from one task to another, attacking his bushes with an electric hedge clipper. It made a fierce buzzing noise.

He worked at the task all week. On Monday he turned a sprawling forsythia bush into a cube. On Tuesday an untidy hydrangea became a ball like a scoop of ice cream. On Wednesday he transformed a holly into a prickly pyramid. On Thursday there was an even more savage racket. Mr. Moon was using a chain saw on a tree in his backyard.

Eddy had to bellow to be heard. "Hey, Uncle Fred, come look!"

His uncle came to the window just in time to see an oak tree tip and crash to the ground. The house shook. In the kitchen the hanging teacups rattled, and in the front hall Henry's plaster eyes widened in surprise.

For a moment the racket stopped, but then the chattering roar began again as the vibrating teeth of Mr. Moon's powerful saw bit into the rough bark of a maple tree.

Eddy shook his uncle's arm and shouted, "We've got to stop him!"

But Uncle Fred only shook his head sadly. "We can't interfere. You know the old saying, Eddy, A man's house is his castle."

"His castle!" gasped Eddy. "But look at him now, Uncle Fred. He's going after the pine tree. It must be against the law."

"No, Eddy, I'm afraid not." Uncle Fred looked wretched. "He can do whatever he wants with his own property."

Eddy couldn't believe it. As the screaming noise of the saw began again, he cried, "I'll make him stop." He plunged away from the window and threw open the back door.

Uncle Fred called after him sharply, "Eddy!"

Eddy slowed down and looked back. "Well, okay, Uncle Fred. I won't say a word. I'll just watch."

And he did. Eddy stood watching all afternoon beside the chicken yard while the flustered hens squawked at the hideous noise, and the cross-eyed cat yowled and crawled under Eddy's bed, and in the kitchen Uncle Fred and Aunt Alex winced and covered their ears.

Watching the destruction, Eddy thought bitterly, *Our hero's sword is frozen in its scabbard.* Leaning over the fence, he glowered at the man with the chain saw. Mr. Moon gave him a quick glance and went right on demolishing one tree after another.

A birch tree sagged and sprawled. Eddy clenched his fists and kept his mouth shut, but when the saw began whining into a flowering dogwood tree, he shouted, "Stop!"

Mr. Moon paid no attention. His saw went right on grinding through the slender trunk, and in a few seconds the dogwood drooped and fell, its blossoming branches thrashing the ground.

It was horrible. As the chain saw ripped its way through the rest of Mr. Moon's trees, Eddy tried to tell himself that this mass murder was perfectly legal by right of some document signed and sealed by the Great and General Court of Massachusetts.

But it was like watching an execution. Mortimer Moon's backyard had become a wilderness of stumps. When the last blossoming lilac lay on the ground, Mr. Moon walked firmly toward his back door, stepping high over the mangled limbs of his fallen trees. At the last minute he saluted Eddy with a cheerful wave.

Sick at heart, Eddy stumbled away. He glanced

at the windows of the house next door, wondering what Miss Stuck-up thought about the slaughter. But all the windows were dark. (It didn't occur to Eddy that someone might be standing behind the curtains in the northwest bedroom on the second floor.)

In the meantime—*ouch*—he tripped over a bump in the lawn and fell to his knees.

Crawling closer, he looked at the little swelling in the grass. Before his eyes it was growing bigger. Something was pushing up from below.

6

THE LEAFY STICK

IT'S SOME SMALL animal, thought Eddy, *like maybe a mole.*

But it wasn't a mole, it was a little stick.

The stick pushed its way upward, growing two inches all at once. Crumbs of dirt fell away around it. Then it paused, and two leaves popped out at the top.

It's a weed, decided Eddy, *some kind of really powerful weed.* Sitting back on his heels, he watched the stick surge up again and fling out four more leaves.

It was nice. He liked it. The leafy stick might be

a weed, but it was the opposite of what was happening next door. Instead of death, it was life. Maybe it came from some jungle in Brazil where everything boiled up out of the forest floor and shot upward to the sky. Maybe some migrating bird had dropped the seed, and now the seed was sprouting eagerly as if it were back in its jungle home instead of way up here in cold New England.   -

Eddy got up from his knees and promised the stick that he would nurse it with as much attention as Aunt Alex gave to her flowers. He'd show that man next door how to take care of a tree.

"Hey, Aunt Alex, Uncle Fred," cried Eddy, sauntering into the house. "Come on out. You've got to see this."

"Oh, we know," said Aunt Alex mournfully.

"It's like a battlefield," said Uncle Fred.

"No, no," said Eddy, "it's something else."

They followed him outdoors. By now the stick was three feet tall, with four leafy twigs. It had stopped growing, but it was trembling a little, as if its jackrabbit start had worn it out.

, "Good heavens," said Aunt Alex. "That wasn't

there yesterday."

"Of course it wasn't," said Eddy. "I just watched it zoom up from the ground."

Then there was a cry. It was Georgie, back from her friend Frieda's house on Hubbard Street. "The trees," she wept. "Oh, the poor trees."

Aunt Alex held out her arms, and Eddy said, "I tried to stop him, Georgie."

"I really don't understand it," said Uncle Fred. "I mean, considering who he is, Mortimer Moon."

"What do you mean?" said Eddy. "Who is he?"

Uncle Fred looked at him grimly. "He's Concord's new tree warden."

Eddy gasped. *"He's* a tree warden? But that's, like, impossible."

"But true," said Uncle Fred.

"And his wife, Margery," murmured Aunt Alex, "has joined the Concord Society of Nature Lovers. They take walks and give tea parties."

"Tea parties," said Eddy scornfully. "What good is that?"

Grieving, they turned their backs on the frightful scene next door.

Behind them as they walked away, the little tree rose softly another inch and unfolded two more leaves in the evening air.

Eddy had not looked up, but once again the stuck-up girl was looking down, seeing everything with her clear green eyes.

7

BEING NICE

A NOTE HAD BEEN slipped under the front door. Eddy picked it up and said, "For you, Aunt Alex."

"For me?" Aunt Alex read the note warily and said, "Oh, dear, she's started already."

"Who?" said Uncle Freddy. "Started what?"

"Giving tea parties. Mrs. Moon has invited us to tea this afternoon."

Eddy said, "No kidding!" and Uncle Fred growled, "What a shame! I fear I have a previous engagement."

Aunt Alex laughed. "Oh, Fred, you do not."

"Well, all right then, I'm sick." He coughed.

"But, Fred, they're our new neighbors. You have to be nice to new neighbors."

"Nice to tree-killers?" Uncle Fred looked fiercely at the plaster bust of Henry Thoreau, then tramped across the hall. Pausing in the study doorway, he said, "I'm not going, and that's that." The door slammed.

"Oh, dear," said Aunt Alex. " I suppose I'll have to go by myself."

"It's okay, Aunt Alex," said Eddy cheerfully. "I'll join you."

"At the tea party?" She looked at him in surprise. "But, Eddy, dear, you're not invited."

"I'll just be taking Uncle Freddy's place. Stepping heroically into the breach, as it were."

"Well, I don't know the proper etiquette, Eddy," said Aunt Alex doubtfully. "For one thing, you'd have to wear a shirt and tie."

"I am already," said Eddy grandly. He patted his T-shirt and grinned at Henry's plaster bust. "This *is* my shirt and tie."

But of course it wasn't. It was a T-shirt printed

with one of Henry's most famous sayings:

SIMPLIFY!
SIMPLIFY!

8

THE TERRIBLE TEA PARTY

"EMERALD, AFTER VACUUMING my Nature Center, please polish the cake stand and iron the doilies."

"Okay, Mrs. Moon."

"Now, Emerald, listen to me. This is extremely important. The cucumbers for the sandwiches must be sliced *extremely thin*."

"Okay, Mrs. Moon."

Emerald walked off to the kitchen, feeling in her pocket for the thing she carried with her all the time. Her fingers could almost read the printed words.

*_**

"Here we are," said Aunt Alex, turning into the walk at No. 38 Walden Street. But halfway along the path they heard a crash and a shriek.

Aunt Alex nudged Eddy and murmured, "Let's wait a few minutes."

Eddy protested in a loud whisper, "You mean that's etiquette? Screaming hostesses, you wait a few minutes?"

They scuttled back up their own porch steps and Uncle Fred said, "Back so soon?"

Eddy shrugged and rolled his eyes, and Aunt Alex said, "Just never you mind," then turned and led Eddy back to the house next door.

This time Mr. and Mrs. Moon were waiting on the porch. Mr. Moon beamed, and Mrs. Moon gushed, "Oh, do come in." Then both their faces fell as they recognized the redheaded boy, the dangerous juvenile delinquent.

But Aunt Alex elbowed Eddy, and at once he recited Uncle Freddy's excuse. "I'm sorry, but my uncle is extremely ill. As a matter of fact, he's at the point of death."

"Eddy!" whispered Aunt Alex.

"Dear me," said Mrs. Moon vaguely, beckoning them inside.

Trailing behind Aunt Alex, Eddy glanced left and right, looking for the green-eyed girl, but she was nowhere in sight. Too stuck-up, probably.

The Moons' living room was a shock. "My Nature Center," said Mrs. Moon, waving her hand proudly at the zoo of china animals on the mantel, the floor lamp shaped like a stork, the stuffed parrot on a stand, the plastic palm tree, the nest of teddy bears.

The sofa was cluttered with pillows embroidered with bunnies and kitties. Eddy pushed aside a cushion in the shape of a ladybug and sat down on a teddy bear. It squawked. "Whoops, sorry, fella." Eddy rescued the bear, which glared at him with its shiny glass eyes.

Mr. Moon frowned at Eddy's shirt, which commanded him to SIMPLIFY, and said to Aunt Alex, "You can see how much my wife loves nature. Well, of course, so do I."

"The blue sky," cooed Mrs. Moon. "The birds,

the butterflies, the elephants, the . . ."

She paused to think, and Eddy said sweetly, "The trees?"

Mr. Moon gave him a sharp look. But then Mrs. Moon began fussing with the teapot, and her husband vanished and came back with a plate of tiny sandwiches.

Aunt Alex accepted one politely. Eddy took one too, and said innocently, "Did your—uh—daughter make them?"

There was a pause, and then Mrs. Moon said, "You mean Emerald? Oh, my goodness, Emerald isn't our daughter. She's my husband's third cousin, twice removed."

"And actually she's an orphan," explained Mr. Moon, his face turning pink. "So we took her in as our maid-of-all-work."

"Your what?" said Eddy.

Mrs. Moon ignored him and frowned at her sandwich. (The cucumber slices were far too thick.) "I'm sorry to say she's dreadfully clumsy. This afternoon she dropped a tray of my best porcelain teacups."

"And disobedient!" complained Mr. Moon, his face turning scarlet. "This morning she refused to paint the furnace."

"You asked her to paint the furnace?" said Aunt Alex, taken aback.

"Well, why not? After all, she is a servant in our employ." Mr. Moon's face turned purple. "As we told you, she is a . . ." He paused to sip his tea.

"Your maid-of-all-work," growled Eddy.

"Of course, said Mr. Moon, scowling, his face now purplish black. "We hired her as a kindness."

"As a kindness," said Eddy darkly. "You mean, like, she mows the lawn?"

Again Mr. Moon glowered at him, but it was his wife's turn to complain. Her voice rose again in anger as she said, "And there's another thing. She talks back. Yesterday when I told her to dust my teddy bears, do you know what she said?"

Dumbly Aunt Alex shook her head.

"She said I should send them to poor children in Africa. My own dear teddies! Imagine!" Mrs. Moon laughed wildly and shook her finger in the air. "Oh, I punished her severely, I can tell you."

This was too much for Eddy. He leaped up, knocking over the tea table. The teapot shattered on the floor. So did the cups and saucers. Cream dribbled out of the pitcher and sugar lumps bounced on the rug.

"Eddy, *dear*," cried Aunt Alex. But when he grinned at her and stamped out of Mrs. Moon's Nature Center, squishing sandwiches under his big shoes and pulverizing teacups, she murmured, "Oh, please forgive me," and darted after Eddy.

"I trust, Mrs. Hall," cried Mr. Moon, "you'll give that young man the scolding he deserves."

"Yes, of course," whispered Aunt Alex, slipping out of the house.

Out-of-doors she took a deep breath of the soft June air. Eddy was nowhere in sight.

The little tree between the houses rustled gently, clapping its leaves as if in praise.

***

"Mortimer, not so loud. The girl will hear you."
"She'd better not."

9

THE TREE FROM FAIRYLAND

THE TEA PARTY had been very bad, but Eddy had learned something. The girl next door was not stuck-up after all. She was like that girl in the story, the one who had to sweep the floor and stay home from the ball—in this case from the tea party. Which meant that there might be a prince around somewhere.

During the night, the little tree took off.

When Georgie tumbled out of bed in the morning and ran to the window, she saw what had happened. The stick had zoomed upward as far as the porch roof. Its handful of slender limbs now sprouted branches, and the branches had fingered out into a thousand twigs, and ten thousand leaves were opening and turning their faces to the sun.

As Georgie watched, a small brown bird flew in from foreign parts, perched on the topmost twig, and began to sing. Perhaps, thought Georgie, it had flown seven thousand miles, all the way from some emperor's garden across the sea.

The tree was enchanted, decided Georgie. It was a tree from fairyland.

Across the way someone was looking at her from a window on the second floor. It was the green-eyed girl. Georgie threw up the screen, leaned out, and shouted, "Hi!"

The girl jumped back from the window and vanished, but Georgie was sure she had been smiling.

It was the last day of school. Yellow buses rumbled back and forth along Walden Street, heading south in the morning and north in the afternoon, but the high school and the middle school were both within walking distance. Neither Eddy nor Georgie needed a ride.

After school the sidewalk teemed with kids hallooing and catcalling.

"Hey, Eddy," boomed Oliver Winslow, slapping him on the back, "where's our hero going this summer?"

"Your hero," said Eddy, reeling from the blow, "ain't going no place."

"Me neither," shouted Oliver. "So, hey, why don't we goof off?"

"See you, Oliver," said Eddy, and he galloped home.

As he opened the gate, he heard a hideous noise from the house next door. A couple of men with chain saws and a wood chipper were clearing away the mess of fallen trees in the backyard. At the front of the house Mrs. Moon toddled up the walk with a pink bag foaming with tissue paper. Then the girl named Emerald threw open a window and shook out a dust mop. Later Eddy saw her hanging up the laundry. Still later:

"Eddy," said Aunt Alex sharply, "what on earth are you doing?"

"Oh, sorry, Aunt Alex." Eddy jumped back from

the window. "I was just, you know, checking up on the tree."

"Eddy, dear, you must never spy on people." But then Aunt Alex looked past him, and her eyes widened in alarm, because Mortimer Moon was tramping heavily across the grass, heading straight for the wonderful tree with his chain saw in his hand.

10

IT'S OUR TREE

"H EY!" SHOUTED EDDY, yelling through the bulge in the screen.

Mr. Moon didn't seem to hear. Before Eddy could force up the clumsy screen, Mr. Moon was down on his knees beside the tree, setting the teeth of the saw against the narrow trunk. "Stop!" shrieked Eddy. "Stop, stop!"

This time Mr. Moon looked up.

Eddy could feel Aunt Alex standing behind him like a monument, and he tried to be polite. "I'm sorry, sir," he said loudly, "but that tree belongs to us. I mean it's in our yard."

Mr. Moon remained on his knees while above him the tree stood in dignified silence, not a leaf shaking. If the small brown bird that had strayed so far from home was still perched on the topmost twig, it did not open its beak. "Your yard?" said Mr. Moon, laughing. "I think you are mistaken."

"Wait a sec," said Eddy. "I'll be right there."

"Gently, Eddy," murmured Aunt Alex.

But this was no time for gentleness. Eddy hurled open the back door, leaped down the porch steps in a single jump, and bounded around the corner of the house. Skidding to a stop beside the tree, he said breathlessly to Mr. Moon, "This has always been our yard." He pointed left and right. "I mean, look, that's our woodpile. That's our bird feeder. That's our basketball net."

"I believe," said Mr. Moon, standing up and smiling at Eddy in the friendliest way, "that your woodpile and bird feeder and basketball net are trespassing on my property."

"No, no," said Eddy. "This part of the yard belongs to us. I mean to my uncle and aunt. It's always belonged to us."

"Unfortunately, young man, you are mistaken," said Mr. Moon. "But it's quite all right." He flourished his chain saw at the woodpile and the bird feeder and the basketball net. "They can stay. I don't mind them at all. Now, forgive me." He flicked the switch on his chain saw and shouted over the buzzing whine, "I'll get rid of this blot on the landscape."

Eddy's politeness deserted him. He lunged forward and stood between Mr. Moon and the tree. "No, no!" he shouted at Mr. Moon. "You can't cut it down. This is our tree."

11

THE DANGEROUS WEED

EDWARD HALL WAS the tallest kid in the Concord-Carlisle High School—that is, after his friend Oliver Winslow. Mr. Moon was short and fat. Eddy towered over him and looked down in fury from his commanding height.

Patiently Mr. Moon put down his chain saw and reasoned with the delinquent kid from next door. "My dear boy, you are overreacting. I happen to have a degree in forestry. I know my trees. This one is not suited to the urban landscape. It is a dangerous weed. It will take over unless it's nipped in the bud. You must have heard of the kudzu vine?"

"The what?"

"The kudzu vine. It's a wild invasive weed. It's taken over whole counties in the South."

"But this isn't a vine, it's a tree. What kind of tree is it anyway?"

Mr. Moon looked flustered. "It is not, I think, a native species. I believe it to be a dangerous invader from Mexico."

Eddy laughed in disbelief. "You mean you don't know what it is, and you want to cut it down? What if it's something really rare?"

At this, almost on cue, a leaf floated down and drifted softly to Eddy's feet.

Mr. Moon snatched it up, turned it over, and grinned. "Look at that," he said, showing it to Eddy. "It's sick already."

"Sick?" said Eddy angrily. "It looks okay to me."

"Insect trails, see there? They're all over it."

Eddy stared at the leaf. It was true. A spidery squiggle, delicate and fine, covered the underside. It didn't look like the trail of a greedy bug. It reminded him of something else, but he couldn't think what.

"I tell you, boy," said Mr. Moon, "this tree is a weed. Have you seen its explosive rate of growth? It's a danger to the entire neighborhood. And anyway"—Mr. Moon prodded the front of Eddy's T-shirt—"this tree just happens to be my tree."

"It is not!" roared Eddy.

Once again Mr. Moon dropped to his knees at the foot of the tree and turned on his chain saw. "Son," he shouted, "I must ask you to get out of the way!"

"Never," shrieked Eddy, leaning against the tree. "You'll have to cut me down first."

"Why, good morning, neighbor," called Uncle Fred, appearing suddenly, having been summoned by Aunt Alex. "Can I help?"

"Oh, good morning, Fred." Mr. Moon turned off the chain saw and stood up again. "It's just a little disagreement. Your boy here seems to think—"

"Uncle Fred," said Eddy, "Mr. Moon thinks this part of the yard belongs to him. He's wrong, isn't he, Uncle Fred?"

"Oh, it's quite all right." Mr. Moon chuckled.

"I'm delighted to play host to your basketball net and bird feeder and woodpile. They are charming assets to my property. No problem."

Uncle Fred looked bewildered. "Your property? I think, Mr. Moon—"

"Please, Fred, call me Mortimer."

"I feel sure, Mortimer," said Uncle Fred, "that my nephew is right. The property line is, I'm sure, right here." He stepped forward and dragged the toe of one shoe along an imaginary line in the grass, several feet beyond the tree in the direction of Mr. Moon's house.

"Oh, but"—Mortimer Moon laughed—"don't forget, I have just been perusing the deed to my house. I am an expert on the exact dimensions of my lot." He stepped past the tree and dragged his shoe along the grass on the other side. "Actually the property line is right here."

Eddy stood back and listened as the tactful argument went back and forth. At last Mr. Moon shook his head and gave in. "All right. The removal can wait. But only until we have a verdict from the

Registry of Deeds." Reaching out a friendly hand, he beamed at Uncle Fred. "Agreed?"

After a slight pause, Uncle Fred shook his hand and murmured, "Agreed."

"And in any case, Fred," said Mr. Moon, picking up his saw, "this tree is sick. It should come down. A tree service would charge you plenty. I'll be glad to take care of it free of charge." Then, as if struck by a jolly idea, he chuckled and said, "Why don't I prune it a little while we wait?"

"Prune it?" said Uncle Fred warily.

"You know, like a gumdrop. I could shape it like a big green gumdrop."

Eddy opened his mouth to protest, but Uncle Fred said mildly, "Why don't we wait?" Nodding a good-bye, he turned away and walked into the house. Eddy followed, grinning. Mr. Moon and his chain saw vanished into the house next door.

Left alone, the little tree—of an exotic species from Mexico or Patagonia or Finland or perhaps even fairyland—stood silent while a dozen new leaves unfolded and the topmost twig stretched six inches higher toward the light.

*_**

*"Mortimer, lower your voice. She's around
here somewhere."*

"If I catch her listening, I'll—"

"Just be a little more careful."

12

THE DECLARATION OF WAR

THE TOWN HALL WAS an old brick building on Monument Square. Once a week Uncle Fred climbed the stairs to the office of the Selectmen and sat at a table with the other members of the board to fight for Truth, Beauty, and Justice—at least that was the way he looked at it. This morning he opened the door of the familiar room on his way to the office of the Town Clerk.

The room was empty except for Millicent Jones, the secretary to the Selectmen, sitting at her desk in a dazzle of sunshine from the window overlooking the square.

"Good morning, Milly," said Uncle Fred. "I was just wondering—" he began, but then there was an interruption, a wild racket from the street.

Milly jumped up and hurried to the window. "Oh, good, he's begun already. Our new tree warden, Mr. Moon, he's going to replant the square. Wrong kind of trees out there, that's what he says."

Uncle Fred hurried to the window and saw a maple tree topple and fall. Two men with chain saws were heading for another. Exclaiming in horror, he watched a horse chestnut thunder to the ground and lie still, the tall spires of its blossoms still quivering.

Sickened, he stumbled away to the Town Clerk's office, but the Town Clerk said, "Sorry, Fred, you'll have to ask the Building Inspector on Keyes Road," and then on Keyes Road his old friend Henrietta Meeks said, "Sorry, Fred, the old survey of your property isn't here, it's in Burlington."

"In Burlington!"

"Right, in the archives in Burlington. We'll have to send somebody. Hey, Fred, you know what? The

51

new tree warden was here this morning, wanting to know the same thing. He's your new neighbor, right, Fred? I forget his name. One of the planets, I think."

"Not exactly," said Uncle Fred unhappily. "He's our companion in the solar system. His name is Moon."

"Oh, right. Mortimer Moon. Charming man. He's got all sorts of marvelous ideas about the care of our town trees."

"Does he indeed?" said Uncle Fred bitterly. Then the rattle of chain saws broke out on Keyes Road, and he had to raise his voice. "HOW LONG BEFORE YOU HEAR FROM BURLINGTON?"

"IT COULD TAKE WEEKS," screamed Henrietta.

"WEEKS!"

"TWO WEEKS, MAYBE THREE."

"WELL, THANK YOU, HENRIETTA."

"SAY THAT AGAIN?"

"I SAID THANK YOU," bellowed Uncle Fred.

"DON'T MENTION IT."

On the way home he tried not to look at the war zone in Monument Square, but it was plain that the Civil War memorial would soon be standing alone, the grass around it baked by the sun, the friendly shade of the trees gone forever.

"What on earth is that noise?" said Aunt Alex, running to the door to meet him, letting in the squawking cat, which streaked past her up the stairs.

"Our neighbor is improving Monument Square," said Uncle Fred dryly.

"Oh, dear." Aunt Alex put her hands over her ears, and the bust of Henry Thoreau winced and closed its plaster eyes.

Eddy leaned over the upstairs banister and hollered, "What about the property line, Uncle Fred?"

"It's a standoff. We won't know for weeks."

Georgie popped out of the kitchen, and said, "Weeks?"

"Well, at least," said Aunt Alex, "your tree will be safe in the meantime."

Eddy wasn't so sure. Stomping back to his room, he tripped over the cat, which yowled and skittered down the back stairs.

The grinding noise from the square was like a declaration of war.

13

HALF AND HALF

THE LETTER CAME at last. Uncle Fred tore open the envelope and read the decision of the Chief Registrar of Deeds for Middlesex County.

Professor Frederick Hall

40 Walden Street

Concord, Massachusetts 01742

Dear Professor Hall,

A careful study of Deed #3792770 in the Middlesex County Registry of Deeds makes it clear that the northwest border of your property on Walden Street is precisely 22 feet from the foundation of the dwelling as it existed in 1893.

Yours truly,
Michael J. Morrisey
Chief Registrar

Twenty-two feet? Uncle Fred went to the cellar, found the steel tape measure, took it outside, and stretched it toward the foot of the tree from the stone foundation of the house.

Eighteen, nineteen, twenty, twenty-one—it was going to be close, very close. Uncle Fred stopped stretching the tape, put his foot on it, and swore. The mark for twenty-two feet was exactly in the middle of the trunk of the tree.

Therefore half the tree belonged to No. 40 Walden Street, the other half to No. 38. It was too bad, but surely from now on the tree would be safe from the dreaded chain saw of Mortimer Moon.

14

MY HALF!

"**O**H, IS THAT SO?" said Mortimer Moon, studying the letter from the Registry of Deeds. "How very interesting." He looked at Uncle Freddy. He looked at the tree. And then he said, "I see. According to this legal document, half of this tree belongs to you and half to me."

"Exactly," said Uncle Fred.

"Very good. We are agreed. Your half is your half, and"—Mr. Moon handed back the letter with a sly grin—"my half is my half, correct?"

Uncle Fred paused before saying, "Of course."

"Why don't we shake on that?" Beaming, Mr.

Moon held out his hand.

Something about the bargain made Uncle Fred uneasy, but once again he shook Mr. Moon's hand.

Therefore no one was watching from the house at No. 40 Walden Street when the scream of the chain saw began again. Eddy catapulted out of his chair at the supper table and burst out the door, but he was too late. As he rounded the corner of the house he saw Mr. Moon back away from the tree with his saw in hand. An enormous wedge had been cut from the smooth gray trunk, a gash that reached to the center of the tree.

Eddy stopped, appalled. Mr. Moon grinned at him and said, "My half just needed a little pruning."

"But it will die!" cried Eddy. "The tree will die!"

"Oh, it was going to die anyway," said Mr. Moon. "It's crawling with insects." He kicked at the chunk of wood on the ground. "You take care of your half and I'll take care of mine." Whistling, he walked away, swinging the chain saw.

Enraged, Eddy stalked up the steps of the front porch, where Georgie stood leaning against the railing, her face pale with dismay. Marching into the house, he shouted, "Come look!"

"Horrible," groaned Uncle Fred.

"How could he?" whispered Aunt Alex.

"He's a murderer, that's how," growled Eddy.

The tree itself seemed unruffled. The gash in its living trunk looked like a death blow, but the canopy was as green as ever, dappled with sun and shadow, its thousands of leaves floating free.

Uncle Fred, Aunt Alex, and Eddy turned away mournfully, but Georgie lingered like a visitor at the bedside of a dying friend. But then she gave a startled cry, and the others looked back, because something was happening.

The pale wood of the gash was darkening, the bark around it thickening and filling in the gaping hole. Then something popped out, a green sprout. As they watched, it surged up and swelled into a sturdy branch. But instead of growing toward the house of Mr. and Mrs. Moon, it squirmed around and shot a leafy spray straight at the front porch of No. 40 Walden Street.

Mr. Moon didn't see it. He was indoors in his

wife's crowded Nature Center, watching her unwrap something from a fluffy bundle of tissue paper, a toy bird covered with sparkles.

"Just listen to this, Mortimer." Mrs. Moon giggled, twisting a key in the bird's back. At once it began to shake and whir and twitter a tinkly tune.

"Good heavens, Margery." Mr. Moon gazed at the bird in wonder. "It's a songbird for your Nature Center."

"Isn't it dear?" said Margery, but then she frowned. "Please shut the window, Mortimer. I can't hear with all that noise outside."

The sash came down with a bang, but the melody filtered through the glass. It was the voice of the small bird from foreign parts—the nightingale—singing in the top of the tree.

15

THE SAINTS OF OLD

THE NEW SPRAY of leaves nearly brushed the corner post of the front porch.

Reaching up, Uncle Fred touched a leaf and said, "So it's all right, Georgie. You don't need to worry about your precious tree. There is no way that man can hurt it now."

Georgie beamed, but Aunt Alex said doubtfully, "You mean he can't do anything to hurt *our half* of the tree."

Eddy too wasn't satisfied. "So what if he cuts the whole thing down? You know, like the whole damn tree?" Eddy leaned far out over the porch railing and stared balefully at the house next door. "I don't trust him. He'll be out there some night with his chain saw. He'll cut the tree down in thirty seconds and leave nothing but a stump. You know, just the way he did in his own backyard."

"Remember, Eddy," said Aunt Alex softly, touching his shoulder, "you mustn't snoop."

"But he may be right," said Uncle Fred. "I'm reminded of the saints of old. Killing a saint wasn't easy. If you stuck them full of arrows, they refused to die. If you threw them in the river, they just kept bobbing up. But if you chopped off their heads"— Uncle Fred swept a finger across his throat—"it never failed."

Georgie shuddered. She didn't say anything, but she made up her mind to keep watch on the tree every hour of the day for weeks if necessary. For months, for years!

Inside the house, in the dim light of the lamp in the hand of the metal lady on the staircase, Aunt Alex missed Georgie. Looking around, she saw only Eddy and Uncle Freddy in the kitchen. Where was Georgie?

Aunt Alex hurried back outside and called, "Georgie, where are you?"

She found her sitting on the grass, leaning against the tree. "Georgie, dear," said Aunt Alex, "aren't you coming in?"

"No," said Georgie.

"But, Georgie, it's getting dark. Please, dear, come in."

"No," said Georgie. "I have to keep watch."

"Oh," said Aunt Alex. She said nothing else for a minute, because it was clear what was happening. It had happened before, when Georgie had set out on the highway to walk all the way to Washington. Most of the time she was quiet and obedient, but when she made up her mind about something important, she became a force of nature, just the way Uncle Fred said.

It was nine o'clock. The sun was at last going down behind the rooftops of the houses along Everett Street, but the top of the tree still shone with rosy light and rustled as if chuckling at some leafy joke.

"All right, Georgie, dear," said Aunt Alex, sitting down beside her on the grass. "Okay if I join you?"

16

THE LURKING OF MORTIMER MOON

AFTER A WHILE UNCLE Fred and Eddy came out with lawn chairs.

"Oh, good," said Aunt Alex, sitting down on one of them gratefully.

Georgie sat down too, and so did Uncle Fred and Eddy. For a minute they sat quietly, their faces looming out of the deepening shadow under the tree.

Then Uncle Fred leaned forward and explained it to Georgie. "The trouble is, my dear, there aren't enough of us. We can't keep an eye on the tree every hour of the day."

Georgie said nothing, but even in the dark the faint blob of her face looked stubborn.

Then the darkness vanished in a blinding light from next door. It flashed in their faces, like a staring eye.

"He's watching," said Aunt Alex, turning her head away.

"Lurking," muttered Uncle Fred angrily.

"Spying on us," growled Eddy.

Then the glare from Mr. Moon's powerful flashlight blinked off and an even more powerful light shone from a different direction. This time it was the full moon, lifting suddenly over the roof like a balloon. Radiance flooded the tree, and the leaves glimmered like mirrors.

There were other lights too: sparks moving here and there in the dark.

"Fireflies," murmured Georgie.

Then another spark kindled in Eddy's head. "Well, okay, Georgie," he said. "Our hero has figured it out. I know what to do."

"What?" whispered Georgie.

"Organize."

There was a shocked silence, and then Uncle Fred said, "Organize! You don't mean Oliver and Frieda and all the rest?"

"Well, naturally," said Eddy.

"Of course," said Georgie.

"Good heavens," said Aunt Alex.

"My God," said Uncle Fred.

*_**

"She heard! She was listening behind the door! She heard every word you said!"

17

THE VIGIL

THEY DIVIDED UP the rest of the night. Aunt Alex and Georgie kept watch until midnight, and then Eddy took over. He brought along a kerosene lantern and a book, but after a couple of hours the print began to blur on the page.

How could he keep awake? Eddy struggled to his feet and began walking around the tree, around and around, while the moon rose to the top of its arc and slowly declined, dropping at last behind the bushy top of a beech tree on Laurel Street. Eddy knew that tree well. It had always been the pride and joy of the neighborhood, at least until the surging growth of their own wonderful tree.

At four in the morning Uncle Fred's alarm clock went off, blasting him awake. It woke up Aunt Alex too. "Oh, what is it?" she said, lifting her head from the pillow.

But at once Georgie popped up in the doorway in her unicorn pajamas like a sergeant at arms. "Your turn now, Uncle Fred," she said brightly.

He rolled out of bed, his hair in a frowze. "Yes, sir, captain, sir." He groaned, shuffling his feet into his slippers and wrapping himself in a blanket.

Eddy was glad to see the mounded shape of his uncle shambling out of the house. "Greetings, oh gracious deliverer," he whispered, and stumbled away to bed.

Uncle Fred sat down on a lawn chair and huddled drowsily in his blanket until Georgie skipped out of the house at dawn. Beaming at him, she said, "Okay, Uncle Fred, it's my turn again."

"Oh, Georgie, dear," said Uncle Fred, whimpering and standing up stiffly, "we can't go on this way. It just won't work."

"Oh, don't worry, Uncle Fred," said Georgie.

"I'll call Frieda right away."

"Well, then," said Uncle Fred, limping away with his blanket trailing behind him on the dewy grass, "I will await further orders."

*_**

"You've got to do something, Mortimer."

"Agreed. What, may I ask, do you suggest?"

THE FELLOWSHIP OF THE NOBLE TREE

FRIEDA'S MOTHER answered the phone. "Why, good morning, Georgie. How are you, dear?"

"I'm fine, Mrs. Caldwell," said Georgie. "Is Frieda there?"

There was a bustling noise in the background, and Georgie could hear Frieda say crisply, "I'll take that." The phone crackled, and then Frieda said, "Caldwell here."

Georgie explained the crisis about the tree, and at once Frieda said, "Gotcha."

Frieda Caldwell was small for her age, but she

was a ball of fire. In the fourth grade she had taken charge of all sixteen thousand kids in Georgie's Pilgrimage of Peace. She had shouted through a megaphone to keep everybody in line beside the highway, all the way to Washington.

· And that wasn't all. Last year Frieda had been the majordomo of the great Mysterious Circus. She had bossed the whole thing, telling everybody what to do, from the clowns to the elephants.

Now of course she came right over, marching firmly all the way from her house on Hubbard Street. Georgie led her around the house to see the glorious tree.

Frieda looked up, and at once the tree fluttered its leaves politely, as if saying "How do you do."

"Well, okay," said Frieda, "I get it. No problem. All we need is a bunch of bodyguards, night and day." She looked at Georgie and grinned. "Like, you know, a protection society, right?"

"Oh, yes," said Georgie, "that's right."

Frieda frowned. "It needs a name. You can't have a society without a name."

Georgie thought a minute. "How about the Tree

Protection Society?"

"It's got to be more exciting than that." Frieda had been reading some terrific books. "Knights of the Tree? No, wait a sec. How about a fellowship? The Fellowship of the Tree?"

"Great." Georgie's eyes sparkled, because she had read the same books.

But Frieda still wasn't satisfied. She ransacked her store of fancy words. "I've got it. How about 'noble'? How about the Fellowship of the Noble Tree?"

"Perfect," breathed Georgie.

"And how about being knights? We could all be Knights of the Fellowship of the Noble Tree."

"Super," said Georgie.

Reverently the two knights looked up at the tree that was to be in their keeping from now on. Modestly the tree stood quietly, as if growing ten feet in the night had been nothing special, as if the thousands of new insect trails in the leaves were nothing to brag about.

But the time had come for action. Frieda whipped out her phone to call Hugo and Oliver, Sidney and

Rachel, Otis and Cissie.

"Hugo," barked Frieda, "we need a Director of Communications for the Fellowship. Right away, Hugo."

"I'm sorry. This is Hugo's father. May I ask who is speaking?"

At once Frieda became the sweet little girl that she was not. (Anything but.) "It's Frieda Caldwell," cooed Frieda. "I'm in Hugo's class at school."

"Oh, I see. Well, Hugo's still asleep, but I'll get him up."

"Oh, thank you, Mr. Von Bismarck. Tell him it's *immensely* important."

"Immensely important. Right you are."

There was a long pause. Frieda frowned and looked at Georgie. Georgie giggled. At last there was a grumbling "Hello?" and Frieda took command.

"Listen here, Hugo, it's brand-new. It's a fellowship. We're all going to be knights. I'll explain at Georgie's. Come right over."

"Now? You mean like now? Hey Frieda, I'm kind of, like, you know, busy."

"Drop everything, Hugo. This is really important stuff."

"But—"

"I said *now*, Hugo."

Over the heads of Frieda and Georgie the noble tree stretched itself taller and popped out a dozen twiggy branches all at once. One stroked the glass of the window where Eddy lay zonked out in bed, while across the way another brushed the screen of the second-floor window where the maid-of-all-work stood behind a curtain looking down.

And from a window on the floor below, another pair of eyes stared at the founding members of the Fellowship of the Noble Tree. Mortimer Moon was making a plan. Turning it over in his mind, he went looking for his wife.

19

THE NOBLE KNIGHTS

W HEN FRIEDA TOLD them to come, they came, and she rounded them up in the shade of the tree—Hugo and Rachel, Sidney and Cissie, Otis and Oliver. "Look, you guys," said Frieda, "do you see this tree?"

They saw the tree. They all said, "Wow," and Oliver said, "Like, it's new, right? It wasn't here before, right?"

Georgie said, "Right," but she too was astonished, because the tree had changed. Only a few weeks ago it had burst out of the ground as a little green twig, but now it seemed hundreds of years old. The leafy top was level with the chimney and the roots were like enfolding arms or caves or mossy thrones, sending twisted fingers snaking over the grass.

"Good," said Frieda. "Now hear this," and she nudged Georgie.

"Hear what?" said Georgie. Her mind went blank.

"The man next door," hissed Frieda. "You know, the guy with the saw."

"Oh, right." Georgie was not used to public speaking. She began in a whisper, but soon the words began pouring out, because the tree was so much in danger. "Mr. Moon owns half of it, you see, and he wants to cut it down."

Then Frieda, who was an old hand at public speaking, took over and explained about the Fellowship of the Noble Tree. "So listen, you guys, we're all going to be, like, knights. You know, Knights of the Fellowship."

For a moment they were too much in awe to say anything. The only sound was the warbling of a bird high in the noble tree. But when Eddy strolled out of the house with a bagel in his hand and said,

"Okay, Frieda, what's up?" they all began talking at once.

"Badges," said Rachel. "I'll make badges. You know, with trees on them." She coughed importantly. "Heraldic devices, that's what they're called."

"How about a tree house?" yelled Otis. "My pop's got all this lumber down-cellar, because, you know, we tore down the old garage."

"Terrific!" yelled Sidney. "I'll help."

"So will I!" howled Otis.

"Me too!" boomed Oliver.

"An intercommunications command post!" bellowed Hugo. "Up in the tree house. I'll wire it up."

"My horse!" screamed Cissie. "I'll bring my horse. Knights, they always had a horse."

"I'll be your page!" shouted Georgie.

"Great!" shrieked Cissie. "I really need a page. I mean, speaking as a knight on horseback."

"Kid stuff!" hollered Eddy. "But okay, your hero will condescend to be your king."

It was bedlam. Frieda was disgusted. She pierced the tumult with a blast from her whistle (left over from last summer's circus). "Hey, everybody, what are we here for anyway? We've got to guard this tree night and day." At once they stopped screeching and looked at her blankly.

Flipping the pages of her notebook, Frieda snatched a pencil from behind her ear and said, "Okay, you knights, raise your hands. Who'll take nine to midnight, Monday through Friday?"

20

UGLINESS NOW

MORTIMER MOON GLOWERED down at the Knights of the Fellowship as they milled around under his bedroom window. The next day he took revenge by attacking with his chain saw the wooded grove along the banks of the Mill Brook across the street.

It was true that they were not handsome trees, but it was painful to hear the *swish-thump-splash*, as one after another came crashing down.

"Oh, Fred, dear," said Aunt Alex, covering her ears, "can't the Selectmen make him stop?'

Uncle Fred squared his jaw and said, "I'll do my best."

At the next meeting of the board in the Town Hall, he complained about the destruction of the Mill Brook trees, and flung out his arms in warning. "Our new tree warden," he said, "is turning this town into a graveyard."

"But all those trees were diseased," said Chairman Jerry Plummer. "That's what Mortimer tells me."

"And after all," said Donald Swallow, the new member of the board, "Mortimer should know."

"Of course he knows," said Jemima Smith. "He has a degree in forestry."

"Mortimer explained it to me," said Annabelle Broom. "All about some kind of beetle and then there's this virus that jumps from tree to tree."

"He says the oaks have canker worm," said Jerry.

"And there's blister rot in the white pines," said Jemima.

"And gypsy moths in the maple trees," said Donald.

"He explained it to me philosophically," said Annabelle. "He said that beauty in the future means a wee bit of ugliness now."

"Ugliness now!" croaked Uncle Fred. "Ugliness for the next quarter of a century!"

"Shhh, Fred," said Jerry as the door opened. "Oh, good afternoon, Mr. Moon. How kind of you to take time out from your busy schedule of—" Jerry stopped, unable to think what sort of things a tree warden did all day, but Uncle Fred finished his sentence by growling, "Murder."

But Mortimer Moon only grinned at him, and said, "Why, greetings, neighbor."

"Oh, Mortimer," gushed Annabelle, "you must explain it to us again, the importance of your crusade. Some of us"—Annabelle nodded at Uncle Fred—"don't seem to understand."

"Well, it's perfectly simple," said Mortimer Moon, sitting down and beaming around the table. "If we don't take out the sick trees, they'll infect all the rest. In fact my neighbor and I"—he smiled forgivingly at Uncle Fred—"have a little disagreement about a badly infected tree right on the property line between us. It's sad, because unless the tree is dealt with promptly, the contagion will spread into my yard. You should see the leaves. They're infested with chewing insects."

"How dreadful," said Annabelle, scowling at Uncle Fred.

"Oh, by the way, Mortimer," said Donald Swallow, "my own trees look pretty healthy, but maybe you should take a look at them. I confess I'd hate to lose my purple beech, but if it's infecting the whole street, I'd certainly sacrifice it, although it would break my heart."

"Glad to be of service," said Mortimer Moon.

Donald Swallow lived on Laurel Street, right around the corner from the professors Hall. Therefore everybody at No. 40 Walden Street heard the scream of Mr. Moon's chain saw and the smashing fall of one mighty limb after another as Donald Swallow's magnificent tree was lopped and chopped and brought to the ground.

Donald stood watching the massacre with tears running down his face. His gigantic beech tree had been the wonder of the neighborhood. With its broad spreading universe of purple leaves, it had been a piece of midnight in the middle of the day.

"Aha, I told you so," said Mortimer Moon, holding up a leaf. "Thrips! See there? All those specks?

Donald bent to look. "I don't see them," he whimpered. "But I'll take your word for it, Mr. Moon."

21

THE MATCHBOOK

T HE OTHER TREE, the new fast-growing tree on Walden Street, was like a city under siege. The houses on either side were fortresses with windows like loopholes in enemy battlements.

But there was a crack in one of the ramparts, because a secret agent had begun to burrow inside the walls.

Mr. Moon's second cousin, three times removed, had been told to beware of the vicious boy next door, but Emerald was beginning to doubt. After watching the delinquent boy and his dangerous little sister from her window and obeying the warnings of Mr. and Mrs. Moon, she had begun to dodge behind doors and hide in closets and listen to their whisperings.

Slowly the world was turning upside down. Good was no longer good, and therefore what had happened to bad? What about the boy and his little sister? What about the other kids who were now swarming in and out of the house next door?

Who, after all, had told her to beware? Her stepmother and stepfather, the same two people who had dragged her away from everything she had always known and loved. Even her cherished family pictures were gone. "Oh, Emerald," her stepmother had said, "I knew you didn't want those dusty old things, so I threw them away."

Only one thing was left of Emerald's old life, a folder of matches printed with her father's name:

O'HIGGINS LUMBER
QUALITY BUILDING MATERIALS

She carried it in her pocket and looked at it sometimes, remembering the bundles of cedar shingles in the warehouse and her father striding between the stacks of sweet-smelling boards.

Instead of a father she now had a stepfather, instead of a mother, a stepmother. But surely most of the stepfathers and stepmothers in the world were kind to their stepchildren? Why were hers so different? They seemed to have come from the fiercest of the fierce old folktales, like the one about the wicked queen who sent a woodcutter into the forest to kill her stepdaughter and bring back her heart.

Her own heart, thought Emerald, was not worth the trouble because it was broken already.

*_**

"You'll have to deal with it somehow, Mortimer."

"You mean like before?"

"Whatever."

22

THE FLOWERING TREE

FRIEDA WAS GOING crazy. Her list of tree-watchers wasn't working.

"I can't possibly do Tuesdays," said Rachel. "I have these really important ballet lessons."

"Monday's out for me," said Cissie. "That's when I baby-sit my kid brother."

"Me too," said Sidney. "Saturday nights I have to keep my bratty little sister from crawling under the sink and eating rat poison."

But after the brutal felling of Mr. Swallow's purple beech—after its dark cloudy head no longer rose above the rooftops on Laurel Street—the list almost made itself. The nine Knights of the Fellowship vowed to keep watch on their own precious tree night and day.

"We've got to get going on the tree house right away," said Eddy. "It's important. We can keep watch a lot better from way up there." Standing high on the mounded roots of the tree, he made an imperious decree. "Speaking as your sovereign, I command all you vassals, serfs, and thralls to get busy."

"What's a thrall?" said Oliver.

"Listen, Eddy," said Sidney. "I mean, oh, sir, forgive me!" Sidney fell to his knees and whimpered, "O Gracious Sovereign, your humble servant begs leave to speak."

"Hear, hear!" shouted Otis.

"You see, Your Majesty," began Sidney, "this fellowship is a democracy. Your Glorious Majesty can't order us around." Springing to his feet, Sidney cried, "All in favor of building a tree house, say aye!"

They all screamed "AYE," and got to work at once.

It was a big job. First the boards that had once been Otis Fisher's father's garage had to be transported to No. 40 Walden Street.

The boards were stacked behind the furnace in Otis's cellar. Oliver and Otis looked at them, and Oliver bulged his biceps and said, "Lemme at 'em."

"Hey," said Otis, "me first. I mean, it's my house." He clawed at one of the mildewed boards, dropped it on his toe, and squealed.

"Out of my way," said Oliver. In the gloom behind the furnace he heaved at the pile of wood, swept up a dozen boards, and drove a nail into his thumb. Dropping the wood with a clatter, he yelled, "Ouch!" The boards bounced. Blood dripped on the floor.

"Oh, my goodness," said Otis's mother, running down the cellar stairs. At once she hurried Oliver up to the kitchen, sprayed his thumb with disinfectant, and wrapped it in a bandage. "There now," she said kindly. "Just be more careful in the future, young man."

"Oh, I will," promised Oliver. "Thanks, Mrs. Fisher."

He thumped back downstairs, and soon he and Otis were carrying armfuls along Everett Street and around the corner to Walden.

Under the tree, the noble tree—which was now taller than the chimneys of all the houses on Walden Street—the pile of boards looked small. But when Frieda inspected it, she said, "Good," and slapped her hands smartly. "Okay, you guys, get to work."

But then there was an interruption. Georgie cried, "Look, oh, look!"

They looked. All nine members of the Fellowship—Otis and Oliver, Eddy and Hugo, Georgie and Rachel, Sidney, Frieda and Cissie, and even Cissie's horse—looked up at the noble tree as it slowly began to flower. Enormous blossoms were softly opening at once. A sweet smell wafted down.

For a moment all of them were lost in wonder, breathing in the fragrance, their arms hanging slack. Above them, reaching out from her window in the house next door, Emerald plucked a flower from the nearest branch and held it to her nose.

Then Frieda woke up and snapped her fingers.

"Hey, everybody, let's get going. Who's got tools? You know, saws and hammers and nails, et cetera? And maybe a ladder? Who's got a ladder?"

*_**

"You mean, the same way? It wasn't easy, remember?"

"This time it's only a girl. She'll be no trouble at all."

23

SIDNEY'S FATHER'S SUSPENDERS

HAMMERS, SAWS, AND nails appeared in a jiffy. So did all the et ceteras. Workbenches were pillaged in many a house along Walden Street, Hubbard, and Everett. Many a father complained.

It took a week of messy effort. Sawhorses stood here and there under the tree. Electric cables snaked out of Aunt Alex's kitchen and looped across the weedy lawn. Hand saws wheezed back and forth, sawdust piled up and matted in the grass, electric drills buzzed, a faulty plug sparked, and Aunt Alex's toaster went *sphutt*.

At last the job was half done. The six parts of the tree house lay flat on the grass, ready to be hauled aloft: the four walls with their window openings, the floor with its open trapdoor, and the plywood roof.

Frieda walked around the finished pieces, bending to inspect them with narrowed eyes. The proud carpenters stood around, waiting for compliments. Instead there was only another command. Frieda straightened up and said, "Okay, you guys, what about those ladders?"

They groaned. But of course she was right. To lift the house high in the tree they would need ladders, lots of ladders.

Eddy dragged a long aluminum ladder out of a tangle of blackberry bushes behind the chicken house, while the bantam hens scrambled in and out and the peevish little rooster screamed.

Sidney's ladder was short enough to carry on his bike. Sidney lashed it to the handlebars and wobbled down Laurel Street, pedaling fast because if he slowed down the whole top-heavy apparatus would tip over.

Cissie's ladder was just a kitchen step stool, but it made a dramatic entrance because she brought it on horseback. Maisie was only a plump brown nag, but high on her back Cissie really looked like a knight.

But then there was another interruption, because Rachel had a surprise. She had been making badges. "Here they are," she said proudly, "your heraldic devices."

They were gorgeous. Rachel had pasted silver paper and green ribbons on pieces of cardboard and fastened safety pins to the back.

Aunt Alex too was carried away. She rummaged in her sewing closet and found a bolt of green cloth. In no time she turned it into knightly doublets by ripping it in nine pieces and cutting round holes in the middle of each piece.

"Here, dear," said Aunt Alex to Georgie, "try this on."

Georgie pulled the green cloth over her head, and then they stood together looking in the mirror, admiring the way the doublet hung loosely front and back.

"Gallant Sir Georgie," said Aunt Alex, smiling down at her. Then she frowned. "It needs a belt, I think."

By afternoon the entire Fellowship was outfitted in green tunics, held together with belts scrounged from drawers and closets. Next morning Sidney's father came down to breakfast holding up his pants with his hands. He glowered at Sidney.

"Uh-oh," said Sidney, but his mother said quickly, "Wait a sec," and hurried upstairs. In a flash she was back with a pair of red suspenders. "I hate suspenders," said Sidney's father, but he wore them like a good sport.

For a while the nine knights strutted around, showing off their new doublets, and Otis said, "It's like we've got armor, sort of."

Aunt Alex looked on admiringly, and then she had another idea. "Oh, Cissie," she called out, "your horse. I've got just enough left for your horse." She ran inside and came out with the last square of green cloth. Cissie tucked it under Maisie's saddle and mounted proudly. Maisie tossed her head and looked magnificent. So did Cissie.

"It's too bad you don't have helmets," said Aunt Alex, "but they're beyond my powers, I'm afraid."

It didn't matter. Even without helmets they felt swashbuckling and brave like true Knights of the Round Table, or better yet, the Fellowship of the Noble Tree.

It was true that Eddy felt foolish dressing up like a little kid, but his huge friend Oliver Winslow slashed the air happily with an invisible sword and Hugo Von Bismarck pushed a button on his antique CD player and a band crashed into life and a singer shouted and a drumbeat rocked the neighborhood, and over their heads the noble tree rustled its leaves almost in time to the music.

But on the ground Frieda was tired of playacting. She said, "Okay, how about that tree house, you guys?" So once again the nine Knights of the Fellowship got back to work, swaggering in their gallant clothes.

In the neighboring house Emerald was busy too. She pulled a chair across the floor to her bedroom window, stood on it, and began unhooking the curtains. They were a fine bright shade of green.

24

MORE ROPE

UNCLE FRED WAS doing his best to keep his nose to the grindstone. His great book about Henry Thoreau and the Oversoul was nearly done.

But there was too much going on. Outside, the tree was like a green village with a population of kids, birds, butterflies, squirrels, and a hundred thousand greedy so-called bugs. And the kids were always spilling over into the house, invading its spaces from cellar to attic. "Hey, Professor Hall," shouted Oliver Winslow, charging into his study, "you got any pulleys?"

"Pulleys?" whimpered Uncle Fred.

"Right, pulleys. Like, you know, they pull stuff."

"Oh, pulleys." Uncle Fred put his head in his hands.

Oliver was big and goofy, but he wasn't stupid. Looming enormously over Uncle Fred, he said, "What's this?" Reaching down with his huge paw, he snatched up a page, stared at it, and said, "Hey, Professor, what's all this stuff about the Oversoul?"

The boy actually seemed interested. "Well, it's a long story," said Uncle Fred, and he did his best to explain.

"Oh, I get it," said Oliver. "You mean it's kind of a cloud up there over the roof, right? Like a power station of good ideas?" Oliver slapped the page back down. "So how about those pulleys, Professor Hall?"

There was no point in fighting it. Uncle Fred made up his mind to let the tide of kids roll over him. He gave up on his chapter and led the way to the cellar. In the dimness he pulled the light string and looked around vaguely, but at once Oliver whooped, snatched up a box of pulleys, and thundered back upstairs.

Uncle Fred retreated to the kitchen, where he found his wife opening cans of tuna fish and Georgie spreading mayonnaise on slices of bread. But there was no peace here either, because Sidney Bloom flung open the side door, his eyes insanely bright, his doublet flying behind him, and shouted, "Hey, Miz Hall, we need more rope! Okay if we use your laundry line?"

Uncle Fred crept back to his study and Aunt Alex looked dazed, but Georgie jumped up at once and ran out to the back porch and pulled down the sheets while Sidney undid the rope from the hooks in the ceiling. Then Georgie draped the sheets over the railing and Sidney galloped back through the kitchen with the rope in his arms, explaining as he headed for the door, "We tie one end to a piece of the tree house, see, Miz Hall?" *Slam* went the screen door. "Then we throw the other end over a branch, and pull it down, and up she goes!"

"I see." Aunt Alex sighed. She also saw the force of the driving will of the nine Knights of the Fellowship in their insane devotion to a wild idea gone mad.

But her laundry line wasn't enough. "More rope!" yelled Frieda.

The knights scattered around the neighborhood, and soon Mrs. Winslow was surprised to find herself draping Oliver's baggy pants over a bush while Hugo's mother hung her husband's union suit over a windowsill and Frieda's father looked on helplessly while Frieda charged out of the house with his best climbing rope. "Okay, okay," he shouted after her. "Just don't cut it, that's all. Don't you dare cut that rope!"

So now they had enough. Sidney's hoist lifted the floor of the tree house to the level of the first branch. Sidney sat beside it, holding it firmly while Eddy attached Mr. Caldwell's climbing rope to Aunt Alex's laundry line and Oliver swarmed higher up the tree and dropped the free end to the ground. Then, while Rachel and Otis and Georgie and Hugo and Frieda hauled down on the rope, the floor of the tree house rose clumsily through the tree, guided by Oliver to a place where three branches made a level platform. There he nudged it into place, and everybody cheered.

The tree house was nearly finished. The Knights of the Fellowship bustled around, attaching ropes to the four walls and the roof, while over their heads the tree waited quietly for the bumpy ascent of five more bulky objects into its leafy crown.

It took another day of sweaty work to snake the cable of an electric drill up through the branches, and drill holes for the screws that would hold the whole thing together, and fasten supporting struts to prop up the floor.

At last there came a moment when the last strut was bolted fast to the trunk of the tree. Their work was done. Balanced here and there around the finished house with their tools dangling from their hands, the Knights of the Fellowship grinned at each other. Their faces were dirty and their doublets torn and ragged, but somewhere overhead a brown bird sang and at the top of the tree new twigs popped out and everywhere at once the hungry insects (if that was what they were) scribbled and scribbled.

"Snacks!" cried Frieda. "Everybody bring

snacks." At once there was a general scramble to the ground. Everybody ran home to ransack refrigerators and cupboards. Soon heavy baskets were hoisted aloft and the booty was laid out on paper napkins.

The snacks didn't last long. Everybody wanted to be up there at once, crowded together, eating everything in sight and enjoying the sense of being high, high up in the noble tree in a cozy home they had made themselves. They looked out on the town of Concord from their dizzy height, rejoicing in the sight of church steeples and rooftops, and reaching out to pick the hard little knobs that had taken the place of the flowers.

Next door Mortimer Moon watched the celebration with glee. "They built it on my side," he told his wife. "Those dumb kids have trespassed on my side of the tree."

"Good gracious, Mortimer. You must speak to Professor Hall. Tell him it's got to come down."

"I've got a better idea. I won't say a word, but I promise you, that shack won't last long."

From his window on the second floor Mortimer had a fine view of the slanting struts supporting the floor of the tree house. They were hefty four-by-fours, *but they were within easy reach.*

25

THE INVISIBLE KNIGHT

MARGERY MOON ENJOYED bursting into Emerald's room without warning to open drawers and look under the bed and pry. This morning she was scandalized by what she saw, or rather by what she didn't see.

"Emerald," she thundered, pointing a furious finger at the window, "what happened to those curtains? Did you take them, you bad girl?"

Emerald kept her nose in her book and said nothing.

"Well, where are they? What did you do with them?"

Emerald turned the page.

"You stupid girl, I'll find them." At once Margery threw open the closet door and rattled the hangers. The curtains were not in the closet, but when she pawed through Emerald's drawers she found what she was looking for. Triumphantly she snatched out the curtains, then gasped in horror, because a round hole had been cut out of the middle of one.

Emerald was punished. Mrs. Moon cut off two weeks of her scanty pay for mowing the lawn, scrubbing floors, dusting furniture, vacuuming rugs, cleaning bathrooms, washing, ironing, and cooking. Emerald obeyed without complaint. Silently she scrubbed and polished, cooked and cleaned. Wordlessly she dusted the Nature Center, fluffed the pillows, and arranged the teddy bears.

She didn't care, because now she was not only a maid-of-all-work, she was a member of the Fellowship. She had watched the building of the tree house, feeling part of it from the beginning, as though she herself had sawed the boards and hauled on the rope, because she too was a Knight of the Fellowship, however invisible and unseen.

∗

"Surely incarceration is indicated."

"You mean as a temporary expedient?"

"Exactly."

26

IT'S ME, THE MOSS!

T HEY HAD ALMOST forgotten what the tree house was for. When the party was over, when nothing was left of the snacks but scattered crumbs of potato chips, they climbed down and headed home—Frieda, Sidney, Otis, Rachel, Cissie, Hugo, and Oliver—because the job was done.

It was lucky that Eddy and Georgie hadn't forgotten. Eddy slapped his little sister on the back and said, "Your watch, right?"

"Right," said Georgie.

"Okay," said Eddy, heading indoors. "Your

kindly sovereign will dispatch a courier with emergency rations."

"Good," said Georgie. At once she took her place as guardian in a mossy hollow at the foot of the tree among heaps of sawdust and a litter of abandoned tools. In the glowing twilight a few leaves drifted down, bumped loose by the lumpy shape of the tree house as it had bashed its way upward. Idly Georgie collected a handful.

Uncle Fred came out a moment later with Eddy's emergency rations on a tray and settled down beside her. "Look, Uncle Fred," said Georgie, spreading out the leaves in a fan. "They have scribbles on the back."

"Scribbles?" Uncle Fred unwrapped a sandwich. "Our illustrious neighbor calls them insect trails."

Georgie held up a leaf in a shaft of sunlight. "But they almost look like writing."

"Of course. Why shouldn't a tree have important things to say? After all, remember the dragon tree of the Western Isles." Uncle Fred took a bite and looked at her keenly.

"The dragon tree?" whispered Georgie.

"The great dragon tree of myth and fable. It's something Henry said."

Georgie thought it over, then asked a sensible question. "What's a dragon got to do with it?"

Uncle Fred thought it over too. "Well, I suppose he meant that making stories is very old, as old as dragons."

"As old as dragons!"

"Of course. Nothing is older than dragons. But stories are just as old. They've been told and retold all over the world, and changed and transformed and turned into other stories. They just went on and on like a growing tree, new ones growing out of old ones until there was a great dragon tree of stories. And also, Georgie dear—mmm, this sandwich is delicious—don't forget that the whole world is covered with alphabets."

"Alphabets?" Georgie said.

"Oh, it's just Henry again." Calmly Uncle Fred unscrewed his thermos and poured himself a cup of coffee. "Another stroke of genius."

Georgie sighed. Uncle Fred was always quoting something mysterious that his hero had written long ago at Walden Pond. Sometimes Georgie saw him talking to the plaster bust, gazing at it as though the drilled holes in Henry's eyes were looking straight back at him. "Oh," said Georgie, "I see."

But she didn't see. What did it mean: *The whole world is covered with alphabets*? After Uncle Fred kissed her and carried the tray back indoors, Georgie stood up and wandered into the backyard to look at the chickens.

They were settling down for the night and burbling softly. Did the chickens have an alphabet? Were they saying good night in their own language? When one of the chickens squawked, was it saying, "Please move over"?

The whole world. Georgie bent to look at a rock. There were flat rings of lichen all over its granite surface. Were they some kind of diagram? An alphabet? Did they mean something?

Slowly Georgie went back to the tree and got down on hands and knees to inspect the carpeting of moss on the massive roots that spread across the grass like the coils of a dragon. Putting her face close, she looked for a pattern in the velvety green garden. Maybe the moss was saying, "Hello, up there! It's me, the moss!"

But of course it wasn't. Georgie stood up. At once the cross-eyed cat bounded across the grass and rubbed her leg. She picked it up and held it against her cheek, wanting to get inside its furry head. Was it saying to itself, "I will now purr"?

But the mind of the cat was as remote as a star. So were the green thoughts of the moss. And if the lichen had secrets, they were hidden deep down in the rock.

27

THE GOOD SNAKE

S UMMER WAS NEARLY over. The sun no longer
rose to the top of the sky. But the thousands
of meandering tracks on the leaves of the tree were
thicker than ever, as though the busy little insects
were in a fury of scribbling.

In spite of the bugs, the noble tree seemed well
and strong. It bushed out over the rooftops and its
broad crown stretched far out over the road. Cars
and trucks moving northwest and southwest on
Walden Street passed through its kindly pool of
shade.

The trunk was now five feet across, and its bark

was as crannied and rough as if the tree had stood in that very spot for a thousand years, as if it had been full grown when Indian tribes moved through the forest and fished in the neighboring stream, as though it were already a tall tree when Parson Bulkeley journeyed into the wilderness to build a meeting house, and taller still when the embattled farmers fired their muskets at the North Bridge, and as if it had been a mighty tree when Henry lived at Walden Pond.

Now it seemed so ancient a thing that the gnarled roots bulged up in hills and domes and folded back on themselves like kneeling elephants, and fiddlehead ferns grew thick in the mossy furrows.

The small green knobs that had followed the flowers had fattened and turned red. Now the bright fruit sparkled among the branches, dangling in clusters from every twig.

In the house next door, Mortimer Moon surveyed the bumper crop from his bedroom window. One of the scarlet fruits dangled so close, he reached out and plucked it.

It lay in his hand, red and shiny and faintly speckled. Was it a peach? A plum? No, it looked more like an apple.

"Why, it looks delicious," said his wife, reaching for it.

Mortimer jerked his hand away, and exclaimed, "Don't touch it. It's probably poison."

"Oh, of course," said Mrs. Moon grumpily. "It would be, wouldn't it?" She turned away, and soon the tinkling tune of her windup bird twittered up the stairs.

Left to himself, Mortimer turned the strange fruit this way and that. He studied it with a magnifying glass. Enlarged, it gleamed redder than ever, and the speckles were golden yellow. It looked so tasty, he was tempted to take a bite. He shouldn't, of course. Anything that beautiful must be dangerous. But he couldn't resist. Sinking in his teeth, he bit off a chunk. At once he made a face and spat it out. It was bitter! It tasted like poison!

From the window of her locked room in the attic, Emerald heard the trilling of the brown bird that had come from far away. She watched it hover and perch on a nearby twig. The dangling fruit bobbed up and down. Emerald reached out, picked one, and took a bite. It was delicious.

From the kitchen door of the house across the way, Aunt Alex came outdoors with a basket and filled it with fallen fruit. Then she took it inside and showed it to Uncle Fred.

He was delighted. He bounded out of the chair. "The tree of knowledge," he cried, frisking around the room. "They're like the fruit of the tree of knowledge in the garden of Eden."

Aunt Alex laughed and protested, "Oh, but Fred, you're forgetting the snake. What about that wicked snake that told Eve to eat the apple?"

"But that's just it," exclaimed Uncle Fred. He stopped capering and smiled at her serenely. "It wasn't wicked. It was a good snake."

"A good snake!"

"Of course. When Adam and Eve ate the apple, their brains began to work. They knew things. They weren't like children anymore."

Aunt Alex looked at the shining fruit in her basket and said thoughtfully, "Why don't I make a pie?"

∗

"But Mortimer, what if she leans out the window and calls for help?"

"I'll screw the window shut."

"What if she breaks the glass?"

"I'll cover it with chicken wire."

"But what about those bratty kids next door? They'll see her!"

"I'll close and lock the shutters."

"Well, but"—Mrs. Moon thought it over—"what if she turns the light on and off? You know, like a signal?"

"My dear, do you think I'm a fool? I'll remove the light bulb."

"Oh, good for you, Mortimer, dear. You've thought of everything. But, oh, what a bore. Now I'll have to carry her meals up two flights of stairs."

"Not for long, my dear. Not for very long."

28

HUMPTY DUMPTY

HUGO'S PRINTOUT OF Frieda's schedule was taped to the refrigerator. "Your turn again, Georgie dear," said Aunt Alex, consulting it. "This afternoon from one to three. Will you be all right? If you need me, give me a shout."

The day was hot. Now that the tree house was finished, there was nothing for the gallant Knights of the Fellowship to do but take turns keeping watch, so today all of them were somewhere else. Then Eddy untangled his bike from the bushes and rode away to goof off somewhere with Oliver Winslow. The only knight left was Georgie.

Slowly she began the long climb to the tree house, moving up from the first ladder to the stout branches that spiraled up and around the massive trunk, reaching all the way to Cissie's mother's step stool, the grand approach to the trapdoor in the floor of the tree house.

Nimbly Georgie crawled through the opening, then made her way across the floor to the sunlit square of the window. Below her through gaps in the leaves she could see Cissie's horse drowsing on the grass with lowered head. Mr. Moon was not marching out of his house with a chain saw, although if Georgie had looked higher, she might have seen a flicker of movement in the attic window. But she didn't.

Turning around, she settled down on the soft pillows that Rachel had brought from home. Rachel had wanted to bring the velvet cushions from her mother's sofa, but her mother had cried, "Rachel Adzarian, you bring those back!" So Rachel had brought pillows instead, along with a cute picture of kittens to hang on the wall, a low stool for a

118

table, and a pink bath mat for a rug.

The pillows were comfortable, but Georgie was bored. She should have brought a book. Turning back to the window, she rested her elbows on the rough edge of the sill and looked out at the great branch that supported the tree house on that side. The branch was round and solid like a powerful arm. All the apples within reach had been picked and turned into pie, but there were the usual sprays of bright green leaves. Idly Georgie reached out, picked a leaf, and turned it over to look at the insect trail on the other side, the scribble that looked almost like writing.

Then she sucked in her breath. It *was* writing. The scribble was words, real words. Joyfully Georgie held the leaf to the light and read the scribble again.

Uncle Fred had said that the whole earth was covered with alphabets, but the chickens had not known their ABCs, and neither had the moss nor the rock nor the cat. But the tree was different.

On the underside of the leaf, distinct and clear,

119

were the words

HUMPTY DUMPTY.

*_**

"We can't just keep her locked up forever."

"Don't you think I know that?"

29

THE DRAGON TREE

I T WAS NO LONGER a game. Uncle Freddy under-
stood it at last. The silly schedule of tree-
guarding, the crazy routine of getting up in the
middle of the night, the general bedlam and hub-
bub and the takeover of No. 40 Walden Street by an
army of holy terrors—everything had turned out to
be important.

The growing tree that spread its broad crown
high and wide over the house was not just a tree, it
was an enchanted library.

He threw himself into the task of guardianship.
"I'll stand watch all night," he told Georgie stoutly.

Aunt Alex volunteered to do double duty, and Eddy forgot to be heroic. "Me too, Georgie," he said humbly.

And when Georgie called Frieda to tell her the news, Frieda whipped her phone out of her pocket and passed the information along to everybody else. At once they all came running, and soon all the Knights of the Fellowship were clambering into the tree.

Sidney was first on the ladder. He raced to the top and snatched at a leaf.

"I don't see anything," he said. "This leaf is blank." He picked a whole handful and said loudly, "They're all blank." He looked accusingly at Georgie as she scrambled past him. "You're out of your mind, Georgie Hall."

Georgie was undaunted. She stepped off the ladder and took a firm hold on a thick spray of twigs over her head. "Higher, we have to climb higher."

"Okay." Eddy lunged past her and disappeared in a tangle of foliage. "Higher it is."

Oliver was right behind him, swinging up like a chimpanzee. He caught up with Eddy so quickly that Eddy stepped on his hand by mistake. Oliver howled, fell, caught himself, laughed, and vaulted still higher.

Now they were swarming all over the tree: Cissie and Otis, Rachel and Hugo, Sidney and Frieda, Oliver and Eddy. All of them surged past Georgie, but she was the first to find a scribbled leaf. Tracing the scribbles with her finger, she mumbled them to herself, "*'Two of every sort shalt thou bring into the ark.'*" And then she shouted, "The ark, it's Noah's ark!"

At once everybody began snatching the scribbled leaves and screaming them out loud.

"*'The wolf in sheep's clothing!'*" hollered Hugo. "That's Aesop! Remember the wolf in sheep's clothing?"

"*'A fresh west wind singing over the wine-dark sea,'*" crowed Cissie, but then she whispered, "*I don't get it.*"

Oliver couldn't figure out his scribbles either. "There's this monster moving through the night," he bellowed. "What monster is that?"

"It's *Beowulf*, stupid," cried Frieda. "*Everybody*

knows that." But then she was puzzled too. "'Sweet showers of April,' what's that all about?"

"Good gracious me," said Hugo, smirking down at Frieda. "It's *Canterbury Tales*. I thought *everybody* knew that. Hey, listen, this one is really gruesome. 'Abandon hope, all ye who enter here.' What's that?"

Nobody knew, but then Eddy whooped. "I know this one: 'Tilting at windmills,' it's *Don Quixote*."

"Hey!" screamed Cissie. "This one's no good. It's some crazy language. Eskimo? Zulu? This whole branch is no good." Leaves showered down from Cissie's fingers, fluttering through the sunlit spaces below, turning end over end and floating to the ground.

"These are no good either," complained Otis. "Oh, wait, here's one." He stood up, hanging on to a twig with two fingers, and read in a funny snarling voice, 'Bah, humbug, said Scrooge.' Okay, you guys, what's that?" And everybody shouted, "*A Christmas Carol*."

Then Eddy yelled joyfully from his perch high overhead, "Uncle Fred will like this one. It's Henry

Thoreau. 'Old shoes will serve a hero.' Remember that from last summer?"

Now they were all climbing higher and higher, swaying in the top of the tree. "'A white-headed whale with a crooked jaw,'" bawled Oliver. "What's that?"

"*Moby-Dick*, stupid," shrieked Rachel. "But, okay, I don't get this one. 'You feel mighty free on a raft.' What's that?"

"Don't be dumb," said Frieda. "Everybody knows that. It's *Huckleberry Finn*." But then Frieda too was bewildered. "What's this about an apple barrel? 'I hid in the apple barrel.' What's that?"

At once a chorus of voices shouted, "*Treasure Island*," and Oliver said in a squeaky Frieda voice, "Oh, *everybody* knows that."

By now they had had enough. Their pockets were stuffed with scribbled leaves. They were hungry, and the air was misty with rain. Blundering down the tree, dropping from branch to branch, they climbed down and around, around and down, all the way to the lowest ladder, and stepped off at last on the ground. Then, patting their bulging pockets and grinning at one another, they abandoned the tree and hurried indoors, expecting praise and hoping for lunch.

Behind them dangled a hundred thousand other stories, epics of gods and heroes told beside Greek campfires, sagas unfolded in Danish royal halls, ballads sung by traveling minstrels, sacred stories from Hindu temples and Buddhist shrines, animal fables passed down through generations of children in the African bush, holy parables inscribed by monks in faraway lonely places, fairy tales read to children in London nurseries and frontier cabins in the American wilderness.

The tree that had appeared only last May as a twig in the ground and had grown to such a gigantic height, the tree that had borne sweet-smelling flowers and shining apples, the tree that was now a legend in the neighborhood, had turned out to be something more than a freakish giant. It was the tree of myth and fable. It was Thoreau's great dragon tree of the Western Isles.

30

UGGA-UGGA

SPREAD OUT ON the kitchen table, the leaves refused to lie still. They lifted at the edges and tumbled over one another. Noah drifted sideways and changed places with Scrooge. Huck Finn jumped over Aesop, Henry Thoreau skipped across Dante's *Divine Comedy* and settled down between *Moby-Dick* and *Little Women*, Mother Goose sailed around the kitchen and landed on the teakettle before fluttering back to the table and floating gently down beside *Don Quixote*.

"Look at that," whispered Aunt Alex. "They're rearranging themselves."

"In time," said Uncle Fred. "They're rearranging themselves in time."

The nine members of the Fellowship crowded around the table to look at their harvest of scribbled leaves. "What I don't get," said Sidney, "is why some of them are blank. You know, way down at the bottom of the tree."

"Me neither," said Hugo.

"Wait a sec," said Eddy. He struck a dramatic pose. "The mighty brain of your hero has plumbed the depths of this mystery." He looked around, grinning. "How sad that the rest of you are such nitwits."

"Mercy me," said Hugo. "How disgusting that our hero is such a twit."

"Such a jerk," agreed Rachel.

"Such an asshole," said Sidney. "Excuse me, Miz Hall."

Aunt Alex smiled and then, very carefully, she began picking up the leaves while Uncle Fred found a paper bag and Eddy said, "Hey, listen, you guys, do you want to hear it or not?"

"Oh, please tell us, *darling* Eddy," said Frieda.

"Well, okay then." Eddy threw open the screen door. "Come on, I'll show you."

"Hey," said Cissie, "it's raining out there."

"Our hero," began Eddy, but Cissie said, "Oh, never mind," and they all ran outdoors and huddled under the vast umbrella of the tree. Eddy reached up to a low branch and pulled off a leaf. "See?" he said, turning it over in his hand. "It's blank because at first nobody knew how to write. For thousands and thousands of years they could say 'ugga-ugga,' but they couldn't write it down."

For a minute they stared back at him in silence. Then Rachel said, "Oh, I get it," and repeated it softly, "Ugga-ugga."

"Ugga-ugga," whispered Georgie.

"Ugga-ugga," gabbled Hugo, laughing and beating his chest.

"Ugga-ugga," bawled Oliver. He sprang to his feet and bounded around in the rain like a caveman, whooping, "UGGA-UGGA, UGGA-UGGA."

Then they all danced out from under the tree and began hopping up and down and shrieking, "UGGA-UGGA, UGGA-UGGA," while the rain drenched their hair and ran down their faces and soaked their shirts and sneakers, and high overhead, peering down through a crack in the locked shutters of her attic window, Emerald murmured softly to herself, "Ugga-ugga, ugga-ugga."

31

THE FIRST NOTE

Emerald's attic prison was a bare room furnished with little more than a chair and a narrow bed, and under the bed a chamber pot. Emerald leaned against the chicken wire over her window and peered through a crack in the shutter at the crazy kids next door, until the rain at last drove them indoors. Then she sat down on the cot and tried to think.

If only she had a candle, she could light it with one of her precious matches. She could wave it back and forth like a signal. But there was no candle. Stretching out on the cot, Emerald wondered what they were thinking about downstairs, and began to be afraid.

When she woke up next morning, she knew what to do. At once she jumped up and went to the window. Perhaps she could slip a piece of paper through a crack. Reaching her fingers through the chicken wire, she tried to rattle the lower sash, but it was too closely jammed in its frame.

But there must be a hole. There had to be a hole. Emerald moved the chair to the window, climbed up, and looked through the broken slat. The morning was bright. She could see green leaves, a bird in a nest, a flash of butterfly wings. Below the tree she could just make out a wisp of the sandy hair of the professor next door.

For a moment she stood quietly looking down at Professor Hall. Then she poked a finger through the barrier of chicken wire and ran it along the crack between the upper and lower sash. This time she found a flaw. The two halves of the window were not a close fit. Perhaps a scrap of paper could be pushed between them.

Emerald had no scrap of paper. But there were

peeling fragments of wallpaper around the window. She had no pen or pencil, but there was another kind of ink. Bravely she set to work.

Finished, her message was sloppy, but bright and clear. She flapped the scrap of wallpaper to dry the wet red word. Then she climbed on the chair and looked down.

Good. The professor was still there. Quickly Emerald folded the note and thrust it through the chicken wire. Then she worked it between the two parts of the window. To her delight it dropped between them, slipped neatly through the gap in the shutter, and fluttered down and out of sight.

But from the window of her Nature Center on the first floor, Margery Moon was also looking out, staring from behind her purple drapes at the man in the lawn chair under the tree, the stubborn neighbor who had caused them so much trouble. She watched him yawn and stretch. The fool had been guarding that dreadful tree all night.

His yawn was catching. Mrs. Moon yawned too, and began to turn away. But then out of the corner of her eye she caught a glimpse of something drifting past the window, a scrap of paper.

At once she darted out-of-doors and peeked around the corner of the house. Professor Hall was leaning back in his chair with his eyes closed. On tiptoe she made her way to the bushes and groped among the twigs until her fingers closed on the scrap of wallpaper, the note that had been dropped by the crafty girl in the attic.

There was only a single word on the note—

HELP

—but it had been written in blood.

32

THE SECOND NOTE

AFTER THAT MRS. MOON kept her eyes peeled. Often she bustled around under Emerald's attic window with a trowel in her hand, pretending to be gardening. What if the girl were to write another note? What if it fell into the wrong hands?

Then there really *was* another note, but this time Mrs. Moon missed it. When Emerald dropped her second scrap of wallpaper through the broken slat of shutter, it was plucked out of the air by a robin, carried away to her nest high in the tree, and tucked among her greenish blue eggs. Before long three infant birds were sitting on Emerald's desperate call for help. Unfortunately none of them could read.

*_**

"But, Mortimer, we can't keep her locked up forever. You'll have to deal with it somehow."

"I intend to. Trust me."

"You mean—like before?"

"Exactly."

33

THE WILD WIND

T HE STORM CAME without warning in the middle of the night. A wild wind began to blow, pelting the rain sideways, sucking the curtains in Eddy's bedroom flat against the screen. When his alarm clock buzzed he got out of bed sleepily and banged down the sash.

From the rest of the house there were shouts of "Quick, quick," and sharp crashes as Uncle Fred and Aunt Alex ran from room to room, slamming down windows on the west side of the house.

Then Georgie shouted, "It's coming in here too," because the wind was blowing from the north. Eddy ran across the hall and helped her close her windows, and then he plunged downstairs to slam the window in the front hall and two more in the study.

When the whole house was safe from the downpour, there were puddles to be mopped up. Aunt Alex and Uncle Fred got down on their knees with sponges in the front hall. Then Aunt Alex looked up and saw Eddy reach into the closet for his parka. Stumbling to her feet, she said, "Oh, Eddy, it's not your turn again? Surely no one's going to chop down that tree in all this rain."

"Don't be too sure," said Uncle Fred grimly. He stood up and poked in the closet for an umbrella. "It's just when he might decide to do it."

"Sidney's out there," said Eddy, popping open the umbrella. "It's my turn now. I'll be okay, Aunt Alex. I'll be nice and dry in the tree house." He threw open the door, slammed it shut behind him, and plunged down the porch steps into the rain.

Now the wind was blustering from the east, sending a lawn chair tumbling along Walden Street and hurling a wall of water against the house next door. A gust wrenched the umbrella out of Eddy's hand and catapulted him across the sodden grass. In the dark he collided with the ladder at the foot of the tree, wrapped his arms around it, and slowly began to climb.

By now he knew the ascent by heart. From the top of the ladder his hands and feet felt their way from one thick branch to the next. The wind battered against him, but once again the broad spread of leaves over his head was like a giant umbrella.

Halfway up he met a drowned rat. "What's it like up there?" shouted Eddy as Sidney scrambled down past him.

"Peachy keen," bawled Sidney. For a moment Eddy watched Sidney's huddled shape drop through the tossing leaves and disappear. Then he looked up and went on climbing, gripping one branch after another, while the tree wallowed and swayed around him. When he fumbled for the stepladder below the trapdoor, he had to hang on, because the tree was reeling and throwing him dizzily left and right. The branches plunged and lifted and plunged again. Holding fast, Eddy looked up and saw the massive crown lash crazily back and forth. He caught his breath. Would the thousands of storytelling leaves be torn away and lost? Would the tree itself survive? Would it last the night?

Eddy hauled himself up the ladder from rung to rung, and crawled at last into the tree house. The floorboards rocked beneath him, but they were dry, undampened by the rain. Rachel's pillows were dry too. Shoving them out of the way, Eddy crept to the opening in the wall and looked down at the window of Emerald's room next door.

It was dark. All the windows of the house were dark. But then to his surprise he saw a spark of light, not from Emerald's window on the second floor but from the shuttered window in the attic. It was only a flicker glimmering between the cracks and almost at once it went out, but soon another little flame appeared, and then a dozen all together, flaring up and shining brightly.

Emerald had struck all her matches alight, squandering them like the girl in the story who lit all of hers at once to keep warm in the bitter cold. Here in Concord it was summertime. There was no bitter cold, only the wild wind and the sound of footsteps on the stairs below.

34

ESCAPE!

THE TREE HOUSE was a refuge from the rain, but not from the howling wind. The lofty shanty in the sky that had been built so securely by the nine hardworking Knights of the Fellowship was pitching and yawing like a ship on a tumultuous sea. The floor tipped under Eddy and threw him sideways. Struggling to his knees, he floundered back to the window—just in time to see the tiny fires flicker behind the shutters of the window across the way, then flare up and go out.

Then above the roar of the wind there was a clattering crash. The shutters rattled off their hinges and blew away. For an instant Eddy saw the dark window, but then a tree limb thrashed against the rain-streaked glass—and the stories on the scribbled leaves began to come alive.

From Noah's ark the trunk of an elephant reached out and buffeted the window. The rusty lance of a knight in dented armor missed its aim and punctured a drainpipe, but Hector launched his Trojan spear and shattered the upper sash, Aladdin hurled his magic lamp and the Mad Hatter his teapot, Pilgrim pitched his staff across the gulf, and Arthur hurled the sword he had plucked from the stone. Then Dorothy heaved a brick from the Yellow Brick Road (throwing underhanded like a girl), and at last the colossal head of the White Whale rose on a hill of water and battered an opening in the wall.

The towering wave deluged Eddy and threw him flat on his back. For a moment the tree house rocked like a cradle, but then, very slowly, it came to rest. Now the shattering winds and driving rain of the mighty storm were racing northwest over the Green Mountains to toss the dark waters of Lake

Champlain and rouse the people of Montreal out of their beds to slam their windows down.

Eddy sat up and tried to get his breath. But then the quaking began again. The floor dipped under him, the board walls creaked. Eddy crawled to the window and saw someone moving slowly toward him on hands and knees. The branch that had shattered the window next door had become a bridge for an escaping prisoner, the green-eyed girl called Emerald, the maid-of-all-work for Mortimer and Margery Moon, the storybook girl with a broom, the sweeper of cinders from the hearth. But as Eddy reached out to lift her over the sill, a stuttering noise broke out below, and then a grinding roar.

The chain saw belonging to Mortimer Moon was reaching up and ripping through the supporting struts of the house like a knife through butter, severing the planks that Eddy himself had hammered into place with six-inch nails and splitting the braces he had anchored with heavy nuts and bolts. The ruptured braces broke apart, and the house began to droop and sag. The walls tore asunder and the floor slumped and tipped with a shrieking of loosened nails and a bursting of snapped bolts.

Emerald gave a cry. Eddy held her and they fell together, while above them the scream of the chain saw died away. Softly Mortimer Moon closed the window of his bedroom and vanished in the dark.

35

THE WRONG PRINCESS

WITH THE END of the storm, the clouds parted and a lopsided moon rose from a bank of cloud. As if a drop cloth were lifted from the town of Concord, three church steeples appeared among the silvery rooftops. Patches of moonlight filtered through the leaves and shone on the broken boards littering the ground and on the girl and the boy who had fallen through the tree.

Afterwards Eddy remembered what had flashed through his mind. Were they falling at the rate of thirty-two feet per second per second, the way they should be? No, he decided, they weren't, because

146

the tree kept catching them in shaggy forks and billowing clouds of leaves. Even so, they dropped violently from the lowest branch and landed with a sickening double thud.

Eddy's face was cushioned in a mossy hollow. For a moment he groaned and lay still. Then he pulled himself up on his bloody knees and crawled to the place where Emerald lay on her back in a pool of moonlight, her scratched face bleeding, her green eyes closed.

Was she alive? To his relief, Eddy saw the front of her shirt—it was green like a knightly tunic—lift and fall. She was breathing, she was alive, she was only sleeping. But perhaps it was the kind of sleep from which she might never wake up.

Then Eddy remembered another of the fairy tales about miscellaneous princesses in various kinds of trouble. Perhaps he had been thinking of the wrong one all this time. What if Emerald were not Cinderella after all? What if she were the princess who fell asleep for a hundred years?

If so, then the story had a simple cure, an easy way to wake her up.

Eddy knelt and tried it, and it worked. Emerald's eyes opened wide. They were green, just the way Georgie had said. She blinked, and said, "Oh," and sat up.

Eddy sat back on his heels, feeling a blush spread over his face from ear to ear. What was the right thing to say to a storybook princess? Should he try his wake-up system a second time? But then before Eddy could decide what to do, a racket broke out next door. There were shouts and curses and scufflings. Doors slammed. Something thundered down the stairs. Then the door for No. 38 Walden Street burst open.

"Mortimer, I have to go back," whimpered Margery. "I forgot my bears." A porcelain chipmunk slipped from her fingers and smashed on the porch floor. Her windup bird came apart in an explosion of clockwork springs. When she stepped on the hem of her flouncy nightgown, she sat down with a thump.

"Never mind your damn bears," snarled Mortimer. His arms were full of coats and pants, but he had to dump them on the grass because his wife refused to budge. Emerald and Eddy watched Mortimer drag Margery to the car, shove her in the backseat, and wedge himself behind the wheel.

As the car zoomed away in the direction of Route 2, one of Mortimer's neckties frisked into the air and draped itself over a telephone wire, a ladybug pillow flew across the road into the Mill Brook, and a shiny black shoe bounced into Aunt Alex's chicken yard, where the little rooster squawked in outrage, demanding to know what in tarnation was going on.

36

THE APPLE BARREL

THE KITCHEN WAS slatted with dawn light. It bounced off the toaster and danced on Georgie's unicorn pajamas, and glowed on Uncle Freddy's scarlet bathrobe, and quivered on the green doublet that Emerald had cut from a curtain, and sparkled on the dot of gold in Eddy's left ear. When the toaster clanged and popped up two slices of bread, Aunt Alex jumped up and cried, "Emerald, more toast? More jam, dear Emerald?"

But Emerald shook her head. She was too eager to tell her story. Her face had been torn by bristling twigs and her left side was bruised from shoulder to knee, but she looked around the table and laughed. She had seen only the tops of their heads before, the man and the woman and the little girl. But she had clearly seen the intent face of the redheaded boy whenever he climbed high in the tree with tools in his pockets.

"I was polishing the silver," began Emerald, but then she was overcome with another burst of laughter. Of course there had been terrible danger and she had been horribly afraid, but all that was over now. Laughing felt strange and new, and she couldn't stop.

"My dear," said Aunt Alex, looking at her with concern, "you're overexcited. Surely you should lie down."

"No, no," said Emerald. "Really, Mrs. Hall, I'm fine." She started her story again. "I was polishing the silver in the pantry and I heard them talking in the kitchen. I was afraid they'd open the door and see me, but they didn't, and I heard everything they said."

"Like the boy in the apple barrel," said Georgie, beaming at Emerald.

"Apple barrel?" Uncle Fred was bewildered. "What apple barrel?"

"Oh, you know, Uncle Freddy," said Georgie. "Remember in *Treasure Island* when Jim was in the apple barrel and he heard the pirates, and they didn't know he was there?"

"Oh, Georgie, kindly shut up," said Eddy.

But Emerald smiled at her and said, "Yes, it was just like that." Then she stopped smiling and twisted her hands in her lap. "After that I listened on purpose."

"Listened to what?" said Eddy. "What did they say?"

"Eddy, dear," said Aunt Alex sternly, "I do think that people who have fallen out of trees should lie down and rest." She shook her head, astonished. "I can't believe neither of you broke a bone. I mean, you fell so far."

"Not really far," said Eddy, who had figured it out. "The tree kept catching us. We didn't fall, we just sort of slithered."

"I'm not really hurt at all," said Emerald. "Well, except for a bump on the head." Gingerly she touched the lump under her hair.

"Oh my dear girl, thank goodness," said Aunt Alex.

Emerald had stopped laughing. Soberly she went on with her story. "Before long I heard about the terrible things my stepfather had done."

"What things?" said Eddy quickly.

"Killing people." Emerald felt in her pocket for the empty folder of matches. "He killed my father."

At this Uncle Fred, Aunt Alex, and Georgie fell silent. Eddy leaned back in his chair and gazed at the green-eyed girl with yellow hair, the sleeping princess he had awakened by a trick from a story-book.

37

POOR LITTLE MORTIMER

AFTERWARDS UNCLE FRED pieced it all together, not only from what Emerald had said, but from things that came out later— newspaper reports and bitter confessions—after Mortimer was at last tracked down.

It was the usual pitiful story. Mortimer complained that it was all the fault of a father who had slapped and beaten him. There had been no way for poor little Mortimer to fight back. He could only stumble away and kick the dog.

No, instead of lavishing affection on his miserable little son, Mortimer's father had loved trees—

trees in the woods, trees in the city, trees in the countryside. And he had doted on one tree more than all the rest, the magnificent maple tree that shaded his house. Mortimer's father had been photographed beside it again and again.

There were no photographs of Mortimer's timid mother, nor any of Mortimer. Instead there were endless pictures of the maple tree in every season of the year, in the delicate leafage of spring and the rich green foliage of summer, in the blazing colors of autumn and white with snow in winter.

Mortimer had grown up in the shadow of the tree, hating and resenting it. Then one day when a crew of men appeared in the woods to clear a trail, his resentment found an outlet. He watched as the screaming chain saws toppled all the pines and oak trees in the way of a power line. Now the proud trees were nothing but trash to be hauled away.

That night Mortimer crept out of his father's house and stumbled up the hill to the place where the men had left their heavy machines. Aiming his flashlight this way and that, he pounced on a chain saw in the back of a truck and carried it, exulting, back down the hill to the tree that rose in front of the house, spreading far and wide its universe of leaves. Then, lifting the powerful saw, he set its savage teeth against the bark and pressed the switch. Bracing himself with all his might, he crouched over the heavy chattering machine as it screamed its way to the other side. And then, while his father sprang out of bed and scrambled to the window and bellowed in rage as his beloved tree trembled and pitched sideways and floundered to the ground, Mortimer fled.

It was the first of many runnings away. For the next ten years Mortimer moved from one New England town to another, showing up in fresh new places, oozing friendliness and goodwill. In one of the towns he met a pretty woman named Margery, just married to a widower with a young daughter. It turned out that Margery's new husband, Jack O'Higgins, was the owner of a lumber yard. But then one day—how sad!—poor Jack was careless with a chain saw, and suddenly Margery O'Higgins became a widow. Oh, how she had wept as she ran away with Mortimer Moon! And, oh, how kind she had been to bring along Jack's orphaned daughter, Emerald! And, oh, how ungrateful that wretched child turned out to be! How stubborn and embarrassing!

Embarrassing? Yes, dreadfully embarrassing, because Jack O'Higgins had left everything to Emerald, not Margery. Stubborn? Oh, yes, the crafty child was horribly stubborn, refusing to sign a simple piece of paper, an ordinary transfer of property from child to guardian. Therefore the tiresome girl had to be dragged along wherever they went, from one town to another, in the hope that sooner or later she could be induced to write her name.

Little by little Uncle Freddy uncovered the long and sorry history of their travels. He learned that Mortimer Moon had been hired by the public works departments of three New England towns, one after another. Each time he had turned up at just the right moment when the town fathers were desperate for a new tree warden. Why? Because the old one had suddenly died. And each time—how strange!—no sooner did Mortimer take over the job than the trees in the public parks began to disappear. In all three towns it had taken the Selectmen a few weeks to notice what was happening. Then of course, too late, they threw him out on his ear.

Emerald told the rest of the miserable story to Uncle Freddy and Eddy as they sat on folding chairs in the dim transcendental air of the old schoolroom.

"I didn't begin listening behind doors until this summer," murmured Emerald, gazing through the door into the hall, where the bust of Henry Thoreau seemed to be cocking his plaster ears. "And then I heard my stepfather brag about what he had done to those poor men in Granite Falls and Mohawk and Tansyville. When I heard him snickering about the clever way he had killed my father, I couldn't stand it. I screamed, and they threw open the door and found me."

Eddy's freckled sunburned face turned pale. Grimly he whispered, "So then they locked you in the attic."

"And after that, my dear," said Uncle Freddy softly, "you were in terrible danger."

Emerald laughed. "But then the storm saved me, and so did the tree."

The storm and the tree? Was that all? Eddy opened his mouth to say something, and then closed it again.

"And of course," said Emerald quickly, grinning at him, "so did Eddy."

38

WICKEDNESS OVERLOAD

AND THEREFORE Emerald O'Higgins, the former maid-of-all-work for Mr. and Mrs. Moon, was free to settle down with the family at No. 40 Walden Street. When high school began in September she walked down the road with Eddy and enrolled in the junior class.

"Hey, you guys, guess what?" hollered Oliver Winslow, spreading the news. "Eddy Hall's got a girlfriend."

Eddy just laughed, and Emerald blushed and pretended not to hear. On the first day of school the gym teacher handed her a hockey stick, and she began racing up and down a sunny field with a bunch of other girls. And then the music teacher presented her with a trombone. "Oh, sorry," protested Emerald, "I don't know how to play the trombone." But Mr. Orth said there was nothing to it, she would catch on right away.

At home she worried about the empty house next door. "What will happen to it?" she asked Uncle Fred. "I mean, it belongs to Mr. and Mrs. Moon, but they've run away. What if they come back?"

"They'll never come back," said Uncle Fred.

"It's your house now," said Aunt Alex. "After all, you're next of kin."

"My house!" Emerald thought of the rooms she had cleaned, the floors she had scrubbed, the attic where she had been imprisoned. "But I don't want it," she said quickly. "I don't want that house at all."

"Then you must sell it," said Uncle Fred.

"I'll call the real estate person," said Aunt Alex. "I forget her name."

Of course it was Annabelle Broom. Annabelle

came at once. But then she was dismayed to hear that it was not No. 40 Walden Street that was for sale, but the house next door.

"Oh, I'm dreadfully sorry," said Annabelle, snatching up her pocketbook. "You'll have to call another realtor. When it's a matter of wickedness overload, my firm wants nothing to do with it."

39

THE GRAND OLD TREE

BY THIS TIME THE enormous tree was famous all over New England. All over the world! Botanists came from near and far to study it.

One was the famous Princeton professor Aristotle Socrates Teasdale. Professor Teasdale crawled around the tree and clambered over the massive roots. "A new species, I think," he said, inspecting a twig with a magnifying glass. "I shall call it *Arborea teasdaliana*."

"Vy, no," said Professor Donkbinkel from the University of Zurich, peering at the rugged bark. "Ziss tree iss zhurely a new zort of valnut." He coughed modestly. "Let uz name it *Arborea donkbinklia.*"

"I'm sorry, gentlemen," said Uncle Fred, "but both of you are wrong. This tree is none other than *Arborea paradisa.*"

"Vot?" said Professor Donbinkel.

"The tree of paradise," explained Uncle Fred.

"How ridiculous," said Professor Teasdale.

"How abzurd," said Professor Donkbinkel.

The three of them huddled among the mossy roots in heated argument while over their heads the tree seemed contented to be itself, whatever that might be.

In October it littered the neighborhood with acorns. One fell in the front yard of Donald Swallow and buried itself in the grass near the stump of his old beech tree.

Next day, while Mr. Swallow was raking leaves in his front yard, he noticed a swelling in the ground. "Goodness me," he said, "that wasn't here before." Then to his astonishment the little mound burst open and a tiny sprig popped up, unfolding a pair of fresh green leaves.

Other acorns fell in Monument Square and along the banks of the Mill Brook. Soon the whole town of Concord was once again bushy and green with trees.

But the tallest and most magnificent was the Dragon Tree. On a warm day in Indian summer, Eddy and Emerald climbed all the way to the top. From there they could see the whole broad country-side.

"Look," said Eddy, pointing south, "there's Walden Pond."

"And the ocean," said Emerald, pointing east.

"And church steeples all over the place," said Eddy, waving his arms north, south, east, and west.

Then, *pop*, there was a small explosion. Looking up, they saw a spray of leaves erupt from the top-most twig. Then another and another.

"More stories," said Emerald wisely, starting down.

"Right," said Eddy, groping for a lower foothold. "People never stop writing stories."

From her bedroom window Georgie watched them move slowly down from branch to branch.

She sucked her pencil as they slid to the ground. She heard the bang of the front door as they walked into the house.

Georgie could not see the metal lady on the newel post smile down at Emerald. Nor could she see the bust of Henry wink one of his plaster eyes at Eddy. She was too busy gazing out her window at the grand old tree as the freshening breeze ruffled its leaves, showering the ground with a carpet of gold.

All summer long the tree had grown past her window, stretching taller and wider against the sky. For months it had been her green and growing neighbor. Therefore her story began in the only way it possibly could—

Once upon a time there was a tree.